KHON'TOR'S WRATH

WRAK-AYYA: THE AGE OF SHADOWS
BOOK ONE

LEIGH ROBERTS

DRAGON WINGS PRESS

CONTENTS

Chapter 1	1
Chapter 2	7
Chapter 3	29
Chapter 4	37
Chapter 5	55
Chapter 6	83
Chapter 7	101
Chapter 8	121
Chapter 9	143
Chapter 10	159
Chapter 11	169
Chapter 12	193
Chapter 13	225
Chapter 14	247
Chapter 15	277
Please Read	303
Acknowledgments	305

Editing by Joy Sephton http://www.justemagine.biz
Cover design by Cherie Fox http://www.cheriefox.com

Sexual activities or events in this book are intended for adults.

ISBN: 978-1-951528-04-1 (ebook)
ISBN: 978-1-951528-01-0 (paperback)

For everyone who ever looked up at the night sky and wondered,

What If?

CHAPTER 1

Only a fool is never afraid, and Khon'Tor, Leader of the largest tribe in the region, was no fool.

Khon'Tor shuddered as a chill crawled up his spine. And the longer Kuruk'Kahn the Overseer spoke, the higher Khon'Tor's anxiety rose.

The other tribal Leaders around the High Council circle shifted in their positions on the cold boulders. If an Adik'Tar as great as Khon'Tor was worried, they would be wise to be worried also.

Adia stood at her favorite rocky high point and looked out across the valley and the verdant hills below. Color was beginning to dust the lower branches of the bushes and deciduous trees. The grasses had started dying back, revealing brown tips.

Goldenseal bloomed everywhere though more than enough had recently been harvested, the seeds set aside for planting in the spring. Everything signaled that fall was coming—a busy time of gathering and preparation for the cold, barren season which would not be far behind.

A warm early morning breeze rustled her long dark hair, bringing with it the fragrance of the wildflowers still in bloom. The scent of deer and elk mingled with others rising from the river below. Adia shielded her eyes with her palm, looking up at several hawks circling overhead, their sharp cries splitting the silence. Etera was alive with beauty, and for the moment, the unrest that had been pricking the back of her mind was silenced. She stood a while yet, enjoying the view before returning to the People. Holding Second Rank, just below the People's Leader, Khon'Tor, her position as Healer was one of power, visibility, and service. And with Khon'Tor still away at a High Council meeting, she knew her presence comforted their community.

But dark clouds of change were hovering, and Adia had been filled with dread for some time. She feared that the topic of the High Council meeting and the source of her uneasiness were connected. The sense of foreboding, which she had not been able to shake for very long, seeped back in, ruining what had been a peaceful moment.

There had been many Healers through the history of the People, but none quite like Adia. Adia's huge heart had won her a special connection with the People, and both genders respected her compassion and wisdom. The Healers of the other tribes revered her and sought out her counsel; even the Medicine Woman of their neighbors, the Brothers.

Except for one dark period ages before—the Wrak-Wavara—the People enjoyed a mutually beneficial long-term relationship with the Brothers and had lived in harmony for generations. Knowledge of the time of Wrak-Wavara was handed down only to the Leaders, the Adik'Tars, within each community and was never discussed openly, even at High Council meetings.

As far back as the Age of the Ancients, the People had lived at peace with the Great Spirit. The People only took what they needed from the land, the animals, and the elements, and they gave back by replenishing where they could. Ancient, reverent, they were governed by the First and Second Laws.

Adia picked her way down the rocky path back to Kthama, the home of her people, established long ago by the Ancients in a mammoth labyrinth of underground caves. Though not all the communities of the People sheltered underground, hers did, and each subsequent generation over the ages made modifications and improvements to the expansive, winding underground caverns to suit their particular needs.

The opening widened into a large cave called the Great Entrance. Stalactites overhead dripped moisture from the sixty-foot ceiling. Past the Great Entrance was the Great Chamber; equally vast, it was large enough to hold all the members of her community, and more, at one time. During cold weather, her people gathered there to share in group activities for which there was no time during the other busy seasons.

Adia passed through the Great Chamber and into the tunnel that led to the Healer's Quarters, where she lived, worked, recharged, and found solitude. She often shared her quarters with her Helper, Nadiwani. Nadiwani was a kindred soul with whom Adia shared a bond beyond their formal relationship as Healer and Healer's Helper.

Adia opened her carrying satchel and started filling it with the Goldenseal roots that she and Nadiwani had stacked in a corner of the storage area. Though not part of their diet, Goldenseal was highly valued by both the People's and the Brothers' Healers for pain management, treating topical infections, and easing female problems.

Because the Goldenseal harvest had been abundant that year, Adia had asked the gatherers to collect extra for Ithua, the Brothers' Medicine Woman. Adia and Ithua often traded gifts. Adia would already have taken the roots to her counterpart had their Leader, Khon'Tor, not been called away to the High Council meeting.

"If you would just let me deliver the Goldenseal —" said Nadiwani.

Adia continued to pack the roots into her woven carrying bag. "I know you worry, but I will be back before twilight. Stay another night in my sleeping quarters, if you wish. That way, you will know when I return safely."

"It's not like you to leave with Khon'Tor away."

Adia stopped what she was doing. Nadiwani was right, but something was pressing her to go. It was more than the Healer's seventh sense. It felt different —heavier—coming from a source; a different center that she did not recognize.

"I'm sure if anything happens Commander Acaraho will take care of it."

"Adia," Nadiwani's face was pinched with concern. Then she sighed and nodded, "I feel it too."

Adia turned to face her friend. "Then you know I *have* to go."

CHAPTER 2

Adia had meant to be off earlier but for some reason slept past her usual awakening time. She completed her morning routine, then gathered up the satchel and padded through the Great Chamber to the entrance. Nadiwani was still sleeping on her mat in the Healer's Quarters, as Adia had taken care not to wake the Helper with her movements.

After she stepped outside, Adia set down the bag of roots and looked up. She knew by the angle of the Sun that she should have been well on her way if she were to be back by twilight. Before moving on, she scanned the valley below one more time. Ready, she hoisted the satchel over her shoulder and picked her way down the steep incline, responding to the urgency that compelled her to go.

The opening to Kthama was situated about halfway up the elevation of the protective, surrounding hillsides. It was overshadowed by a towering outcrop of rock, well-hidden from those who did not know it was there. The rocky ledges and boulders made travel along even the established paths tricky. Many of them wound dangerously close to drop-offs which opened to Great River's churning waters hundreds of feet below.

Adia finally made it down to the valley floor and stood before the river she had to cross. Heavy rainfall and runoff from days earlier had made the water exceptionally high—a churning mass of mud and foam. She felt that to ensure no unnecessary risks, she must take a different route—one she had not often traveled. *Nadiwani would definitely not be pleased if she knew I am taking the un-established route.*

As the way unwound before her, taking her farther and farther from Kthama, Adia wondered if she would be able to return by twilight after all. The terrain changed from the larger protective deciduous trees and firs of the forested hillside to lower under-brush and eventually gave way to grassy stretches she could pass over more easily. As she traveled, various woodland creatures scurried across her path. Not the lightest of walkers, her approach rousted many from their hiding places. She knew they were there before she saw them, as she knew each of their sounds and scents like the back of her hand. Though she had not often come this way before, the route was familiar and yet unfamiliar to her. She was as at home in the nature of the forest as she was in the home cave.

As she came out of the forest and neared the meadow's edge, a feeling of darkness filled her. *This was her seventh sense, the gift of the Great Mother;* this came from a source she recognized. It was sometimes given to her as a picture, sometimes as a feeling, sometimes as a provision of facts. Like the other Healers before her, she was strongly connected to the Great Mother. Though all the females of the People had this seventh sense to some extent, it was far more advanced in the Healers.

Adia paused as darkness surged through her, almost knocking her off balance.

She swallowed hard. It was practically an auditory message, "*Stop. Look. There is something important here for you. Do not miss it in your haste.*"

Adia stepped out to cross the meadow and no longer had to concentrate on her footing. As she looked up, an unnatural assembly of wood and planks caught her eye. It was an odd arrangement of both round and square—nothing the Brothers or her people would have constructed.

She immediately knew that the Outsiders had built it, but she did not realize they had ventured this far into the Brothers' territory. Stopping where she stood and stooping down, she scanned the area for any signs of activity. As she knelt, the wind shifted, and a stench of blood filled her nostrils. *Not good. Not good at all.*

She turned her head toward what she thought

sounded like horses pawing and whinnying. The hair on the back of her neck pricked up.

Even if she had wanted to, she would not have been able to leave, despite her clear feelings of dread. Even if she had not been a Healer, and even if she had not been directed by the laws to care for the wounded, sick, and helpless, she was still a female and would not withhold help. Both her greatest strength and her greatest weakness were rooted in her compassionate heart.

Adia crept closer. As she approached the structure, she noticed tracks of the carrier animals that both the Brothers and the White Men used. *But these are not of the Brothers. Only the White Men put hard plates on their horse's hooves,* she thought.

From the traces, she could tell they had come in at full speed, and there had been at least two of them riding together. *A set of tracks going back in the same direction are mixed in with the first. Whoever they were, they returned the way they came—and quickly.*

'White Man' was their term for themselves. The People and the Brothers referred to them as the Outsiders, though they also had other names which loosely translated into White Wasters or White Takers. From what they knew of them, the White Man was a soulless creature who took what he wanted with little regard for anything but his own desires. He slaughtered the woodland creatures, killing more than he needed and taking only their hides, leaving the rest to rot. He also had little respect for the land of the others who lived there.

Adia continued her approach. As she got closer, she pinched her nose to try to block out the unbearable stench of blood. She hoped the wind would shift in the other direction, but soon realized it would not have made any difference.

As she crept up to the structure, two horses bucked, pulling hard against the restraints that tethered them to it. She knew her presence alarmed them, but she could not leave them trapped. It took her a moment, but after fumbling a bit with the connections she finally freed them, and they quickly galloped off in opposite directions.

Walking around the back of the structure, where the offensive smell was even stronger, she spied the prior occupants.

Brutality was not in the People's hearts. If something had to die, they killed it quickly and swiftly. They never inflicted suffering. And so the resultant scene sickened Adia to her depths. *Clearly, this had not been a fair fight—this was an ambush; a massacre.*

A White female lay sprawled on the ground approximately ten feet from the structure. Her body was crumpled in an unnatural position, and her arms lay outstretched, limp and pale. Bright red pools of blood were everywhere. A large, wide, red gash peeled her throat open. Her coverings were in disarray. It was clear there had been a struggle, and that she had been violated. Adia had not seen any Whites before, but she guessed the female was of offspring-bearing age. The bloody wounds were still glistening; this slaughter had only very recently taken place. Adia checked for signs of life in the female but already knew she would find none.

Another body was lying further away, presumably the female's mate. He had been butchered equally violently.

The scalps had been cut from their heads, and Adia wondered at the contradiction, because it was certainly the White Men's horses which had been ridden in, yet from the little she knew, this was not something the Whites practiced. *Even though they are the only tribe close enough to this place, none of the Brothers would do something this barbaric.*

Adia took a moment to collect herself. She had never seen such abominable acts in her life.

There was nothing there for her to do. They had already returned to the Great Spirit. But before she left, she said a prayer for each of them.

All the People shared the same belief in an overseeing guiding spirit—that there was another life waiting for them after this one. She wondered if an afterlife was waiting for the White Men who did this, though by what she had seen today, they did not deserve one.

Just as she was about to leave, a sound turned her blood cold. It was not a sound of nature, not like the hawks crying overhead or the horses which had been lashed to the structure—it was a sound some*thing*, some*one* had made.

Turning back to where the sound originated, her heart stopped in her chest. This was more than she had bargained for, and her blood ran cold.

The strange structure was covered by some type of woven material which was stretched over it by the use of curved hoops—much as the People would bend willow branches to frame their baskets.

Adia gingerly pulled the cover aside so she could see inside. Her eyes were drawn to the smallest of movements. There, under a blanket, something was wiggling around. She pulled back the wrappings and uncovered a tiny offspring who looked up at her with bright, sky blue eyes and giggled.

Adia froze, though her mind was reeling and her pulse was racing. Somehow, in their acts of abomination, they had missed the offspring. Surely it had not been intentional. By what miracle it had remained undiscovered, Adia could not imagine.

This is an offspring, but not of the People, not of the Brothers—this is an Outsider. Intruders in our land: soulless, selfish marauders who unleash unspeakable cruelty even on their own kind. And here lies one of these monsters—helpless, abandoned, but a beast seed waiting to grow into another as uncaring and cold and ruthless as the rest. Surely it deserves to die as well as any of them!

These cold thoughts passed through Adia's head, and for a moment she wanted to harden her heart with them, so she could walk away and let it perish on its own. It surely would, with no one to care for it. It was clearly not able to survive without a caretaker. *Perhaps it would be kinder of me to kill the offspring quickly, rather than to abandon it here to a long and miserable end? That would be in line with our ways—we never let anything suffer when its end is inevitable.*

She was frozen by the conflict that stormed inside her. The First Laws resounded in her head; only harm if first harmed, protect and heal the helpless or infirm, offspring are the future and are sacred. Did the First Laws also extend to these creatures? Was she honor-bound to save this offspring? What about her vow as a Healer? What about the Second Law which forbade contact with the Outsiders?

Adia glanced down at the small offspring who was making quiet, happy noises. It was frail and tiny and pale. Its only redeeming feature was its eyes, the color of the summer sky. It smiled, then reached up its little hands as if to touch her. Tears stung her eyes. "You're not a monster. At least not yet," she said. *Perhaps you might never be. We do not know if it is their destiny for all of them to become so. There has to be more to the Whites than what we have heard. The stories have all been about the males. Surely the females cannot be like them also, cruel and soulless?*

Heartache swelled inside her, split between her loyalty to the People and her role as Healer. The Second Law expressly prohibited contact with the Outsiders. There was no other way to interpret it. If she did not leave it there to die or dispatch it herself, the other alternative was to take it back with her, directly violating Sacred Law.

Adia made her decision. She could not abandon this offspring to its fate, nor bring it quickly to an end by her own hand. *Second Law or not, you're coming with me.* The moment she made the decision, the pull which had drawn her to come was sated and the feeling of darkness lifted.

Adia turned her satchel over and pressed the Goldenseal down far enough to make room for the offspring. As she picked it up, she noticed it was a male. *Not only an Outsider but even worse, a male.*

But it was too late; her heart had won. She placed him carefully on top of the plants. In the corner where he had lain, she saw a bundle that looked as if it were meant to resemble a brown, stuffed bear. The Brothers had playthings of this type, fashioned to resemble animals in the natural world. She scooped it up, along with one of his blankets and put it in with him, which seemed to please him.

As she picked up the blankets, a small bag of toughened hide fell out and clinked to the floor of the structure. She turned the bag over and emptied it into her other hand. The thing that had made the noise was a shiny, thick, oval shape, made of a hard substance the White Man forged. It was hinged and had broken open from the fall to the floor. Inside was what she took to be a likeness of the man and the woman lying dead outside—before they had lost their scalps. A strong sense came over her that she should take it, so she tucked it into a corner of the satchel under everything else.

Adia started off with her precious cargo, and a heart at peace with her decision—for the moment.

She considered returning directly to Kthama but realized the offspring would soon need to nurse. It was not crying now, but that would quickly change if she did not find it nourishment. *I will have to hope the Brothers have a wet nurse who will be willing to feed the offspring. Ithua will be getting a bigger surprise today than just the Goldenseal,* she sighed.

As Adia closed the distance between herself and the Brothers' village, the gravity of what she had done started to seep into her consciousness.

Oh, Father, how I wish you were still here with me. Though he had been the Leader of a neighboring community, the People of the Deep Valley, her father was remembered and revered among all the People for his kind, yet wise reign. He had kept her close, and she had learned a great deal from him about strength and forbearance, and how to yield one without compromising the other. *Father, how did you manage to find such a balance between the tenets of the First and Second Laws?*

Unfortunately, her mother had died giving life to Adia, her first and only offspring. She was raised by the other females of the People of the Deep Valley but did not have that one, close, mothering relationship which others enjoyed. It had made the death of her father harder to bear, and she cherished her friendship with Nadiwani, as well as with Ithua, Medicine Woman of the Brothers, all the more because of it.

Adia entered the Brothers' village later than she had expected. Ithua saw her and rushed forward while the others stood transfixed at her approach. A visit from one of the People was rare. Ithua saw them staring at Adia, and scolding, turned them all away.

"Welcome, Adia!"

"Do not welcome me yet, Ithua, until you see what I have done. I have committed a terrible crime, and I desperately need your help."

Just as she said it, a cry came from the satchel she was carrying.

"Is that a child?"

"It is a hungry child, yes. Can you help me? Do you perhaps have a new mother with more than enough milk right now? I do not know when he last nursed."

Ithua did not ask questions but turned instead to a young maiden standing nearby, whom Adia did not recognize. "Honovi. Close your mouth and fetch Arina. Quickly!"

Ithua ushered Adia inside her shelter. Adia immediately sat, so she would not tower over Ithua.

"May I see?"

"Brace yourself, Ithua."

Ithua gave Adia a quizzical look as she opened the satchel.

"Oh, Adia. What have you done?"

"What I had to, Ithua. I did what I had to."

Ithua lifted out and held up the baby. He was crying now, suddenly both tired and hungry. Ithua handed him to Adia to comfort just as Honovi returned with Arina in hand. The eyes of both women widened at the sight of Adia, the Healer of the largest Sasquatch tribe in the region, holding a Waschini child.

The Brothers were much closer to the Waschini in build, and though it was terribly pale, the offspring's appearance was less off-putting to them than it would be to the People. Arina reached for it immediately. While the he nursed, Adia explained how she had come across the fresh massacre and discovered the infant unharmed. The women listened intently, all realizing the severity of the crime she had just committed.

Though it had not always been so, the Brothers and the Sasquatch had an interdependent relationship. These women knew the laws of the People, and also knew of their Leader, Khon'Tor. His wrath was going to be considerable.

After a while, Adia decided she needed to get

back. It would be well past twilight when she returned, and Nadiwani would be worried.

"Do you want Arina to accompany you?"

Adia looked at Arina, confused, not understanding if Ithua was proposing the woman bring her own infant with her to Kthama.

"My baby was stillborn, Healer, but my milk has not yet dried up. I would be glad to accompany you if you wish."

Adia reached out to comfort Arina, who instinctively pulled back.

"I'm sorry. I forget our appearance can be alarming. Are you sure you would be willing, Arina? Kthama is filled with People of my kind."

"I want to help if I can."

"Very well. It is within my right to bring you to Kthama. The trick will be to keep *him* from crying before we get to my quarters."

Ithua spoke, "You can stop and let Arina nurse him again just before you get there. And I can give him a bit of chamomile. Let me get some small wraps to keep him warm as that will also help."

The females fussed, readying Adia for her journey home, and before too long the Healer and Arina set out.

The two walked together in silence. Adia's thoughts turned back to the seriousness of what she had done and what the repercussions might be. Bringing the offspring was bad enough, but she was also starting to second-guess her decision to take the offspring's personal items with her. *Bringing an Outsider in is transgression enough. But these other things; they have something to do with who he is. Might they be able to lead the Waschini to us? There are no laws against it, but still—*

The laws had been written long ago, before the White Man, so the items were not explicitly forbidden, but she knew Khon'Tor well enough to know they would only inflame the fire of his anger, which would be considerable to start with.

When they were almost there, she turned to Arina. "Here is a good place for you to nurse him again. I need to take care of something and will return in just a few moments."

Diverting from the main path, Adia took a turn and headed through some heavy underbrush, making her way to the Healer's Cove. This was a place sacred to her and each of the People's Healers before her. Nadiwani had brought her there when she first came to Kthama. It was where they connected with their heritage; their sacred role to the People. All the People's Healers had come to this quiet, hidden, protected place to sit on the soft mosses and seek the counsel of the Great Mother who guided them.

At the back of the cove and partially recessed into a jagged rock wall that ran probably eighty feet almost straight up, stood a massive boulder caked with the dirt and debris of the ages and covered in Bittersweet vines. Other than its size and its peculiar placement, the rock itself had no other outstanding physical qualities.

Standing with it looming over her, Adia felt small and humble; connecting more easily with the Great Mother. To Adia, this was more than a place of refuge. To her, this place held the secrets of the ages; it seemed to whisper to her that there were stories here—mysteries locked away, waiting to be told.

She paused in front of the Healer's Stone and set down the satchel, which had been a gift from Ithua, Medicine Woman of the Brothers, and was woven of sturdy reeds and skins. Unlike much of the Brothers' work, this did not sport the bright colors the Brothers favored. The natural colors of the materials had been unaltered—letting it blend in easily with the natural surroundings; a fact Adia appreciated.

She retrieved the hard, round object with the likenesses of the offspring's parents in it; the locket. *Perhaps I should fling it into the Great River instead.*

But something had told her to bring it, and she had come this far. Wrapping the pouch in leaves to protect it from the elements, she pawed out a small hole and buried it, memorizing its location at the base of the looming rock. And there she left it, in its shallow grave for safekeeping should the time ever come when it was needed.

Then she paused for a moment, remembering the blanket. *Perhaps I should go and bury it and the bear too? But they are the only things he will have to comfort him. I do not see how it can hurt to keep them.*

When Adia did not know what to do, she refrained from making irreversible decisions, trusting instead that the right choice would come to her eventually. It was a movement of restraint her father had taught her long ago.

She made her way back to where she had left Arina, and with her continued onto the main path to Kthama, trying to enjoy the smells and sounds of their land, which usually gave her pleasure.

A sound of footfalls ahead gave Adia pause, and she found a nook to duck into with Arina while they waited. She suspected it was one of the High Protector's watchers, most likely the one named Akule, returning at the end of his watch.

As they waited, Arina cuddled the offspring while, thankfully, he slept off his meal, and Adia gave thanks that Khon'Tor was away. She knew she could depend on the guidance of the Great Mother, but she would have more time to prepare what to say, and how to say it. Khon'Tor was not an easy male to deal with under the best of circumstances. She had clearly broken the laws by bringing the Waschini offspring there—there was no way to avoid his anger. He would have no sympathy for her or the Outsider offspring. But with a careful approach, she might be able to soften some of his reaction. Perhaps her role as Healer would carry some weight in her responsibility to rescue the helpless creature.

A Leader of the People, or Adoeete, held First Rank, and in addition to setting direction and guiding the community members, was responsible for enforcement of the First and Second Laws, the focus always the ongoing well-being of the community.

The challenge with Khon'Tor came from his natural Alpha personality, coupled with his strict interpretation of the First and Second Laws. Adia believed he did have the best interests of the People at heart and was committed to their well-being. But she found Khon'Tor sometimes overly stringent in administering the First and Second Laws, unlike her father.

Adia's position as Healer, the Second Rank, was in some ways more important than that of the Leader. Healers held the profound knowledge of the People, not only in areas of medicine but also in their connection to the Great Mother.

The Great Mother was one of the three aspects of the Great Spirit, the One-Who-Is-Three. Healers were chosen from the female offspring who showed a stronger seventh sense than most. Because of the Healer's connection to the Great Mother, by balancing the Leader's more practical, more detached perspective, her leadership was crucial to the guidance of the community.

This fact would potentially only make her involvement with the Waschini offspring more devastating for the community, and Adia would be relieved when they were finally able to slip into her quarters unnoticed by anyone.

As they returned to the path, Adia looked up at the emerging stars and shook her head. Darkness was almost upon them; but that had now worked to her advantage, though Nadiwani would probably be beside herself with worry.

Soon they entered and passed through the Great Entrance, and then through the Great Chamber beyond it. Though there was only a handful of females left cleaning up from the evening meal, Adia still kept to the side walls, trying to stay in shadow and hoping the offspring would not make a sound. Somehow, they were able to pass unnoticed and slipped into the tunnel that led to her quarters. She was especially grateful she had managed to avoid Khon'Tor's mate, Hakani.

Everything at Kthama was on a huge scale and the Healer's Quarters were also of considerable size. Dried hanging herbs, piles of ground spices, sorting areas and the like filled the space—giving it a more outdoorsy appearance than it really was—a rock room buried underground. Sunlight brightened her quarters thanks to sloping tunnels poked up through the roof; the openings up top cleverly constructed to allow the light, but not the elements to enter.

Nadiwani heard Adia arrive, and already on her sleeping mat, propped herself up on her elbows. Seeing one of the Brothers with Adia, she hauled herself up and padded over to greet the visitor properly.

Adia held up her finger to her lips. She immediately switched to Handspeak, not wishing to make any sound that might wake the sleeping offspring.

After greeting Arina, Nadiwani asked Adia in Handspeak where she had been. The Helper's hands flew, her brows knitted together in perplexity, "What happened? Why are you so late? And why is your satchel still full? Were you not able to deliver the Goldenseal to Ithua?"

Even as Nadiwani was assaulting Adia with the flurry of questions, on seeing Arina, she was once again reminded of the differences between the People and the Brothers. How short and frail they were, and their features so delicate by comparison. Lacking physical strength of any measure, they were fortunate to be intelligent and could compensate for their physical handicaps through innovation. Their small hands and fingers allowed them to fashion weavings, thread bowstrings, and sort and manipulate smaller items in far more intricate ways than the People could.

Before Adia could answer any questions, a movement from the satchel caught Nadiwani's eye, and a small sound escaped from within. Her head snapped toward it. The sound was not exactly familiar, not the right pitch or volume, but it was close enough. Something—or rather, some*one*—was inside the carrier.

"Oh, Adia," signed Nadiwani, her shoulders dropping, looking to Arina and then back to the Healer. "*What have you done?*"

As Healer, Adia did not need to explain herself to her Helper. But Nadiwani was more than the Healer's Helper; she was her friend, and the sister she never had. Their relationship was one of mutual respect, concern, and goodwill. And right now, Adia needed Nadiwani's support and not her condemnation.

"Nadiwani, that is the second time someone has asked me today. Think with your heart before you speak. I need your support now, not your judgment," signed Adia.

The Helper was already kneeling on the cold rock floor, peeling open the satchel. The moment she could see inside, she stopped. She turned and looked up at Adia. "Are you out of your mind?" Her hands were sharp, harsh, and hard; all slicing angles and swift movements.

"Do you *know* what he is going to do to you?" her eyes flashed.

Adia knew there was nothing Nadiwani could be thinking that she had not already grappled with on the way home. She had played out Khon'Tor's wrath many times in her mind. She could bear his anger, but her stomach was in knots worrying about how severe her punishment would be; and what might be the fate of the offspring—her instincts to the contrary.

Adia did not answer Nadiwani, who stood from her kneeling position and walked away, dropping her hands at her side and letting out a huge sigh of exasperation. She turned back to face Adia, shaking her head. Then she lifted her hands in front of her as if to ask again, "Why?" "Why would you even think to do this?" and turned away once more.

Adia waited for Nadiwani's emotions to work their way out. Despite their friendship, she was not going to apologize because she knew in her heart that she had made the right decision. Regardless of her inability to take its life or allow it to perish by neglect, she knew this offspring was somehow important to her people. It was not a clear vision, as others were, but it was not uncommon for information to be obscured when your own path was involved. But whatever else was to be, she knew it was not an accident that she had stumbled across the place of his parent's massacre. And when she had decided to save the offspring, the darkness had left her.

With softer eyes, Nadiwani turned to face her friend again. She sighed. "I understand. I do. *This* was why you had to go. This—offspring."

She bent over and lifted the Waschini from the carrier. His blanket, almost the same color as his eyes, was dragged out with him. It was so finely woven, so soft, with much finer workmanship than anything they or the Brothers had ever produced. It was decorated with little swirls on one corner. From within the satchel, Nadiwani pulled out the brown toy. "What is this supposed to be? Surely not a Sarnonn?"

"Oh no, Nadiwani. The Waschini do not know about us, let alone the Sarnonn. I am sure it is just meant to be a bear."

Relieved, Nadiwani held it up to the offspring, wiggling it back and forth, and he smiled.

Adia spoke again. "Arina will be staying for a day or so until we can arrange another wet nurse. It is late to make a place for her; let us take from my mat and the spare one you use. We can fix them back and make her a proper one tomorrow."

So, the females prepared a makeshift place for Arina, and with the offspring now sleeping, also turned in.

Adia did not welcome the days that were to come.

CHAPTER 3

Though Adia believed she and Arina had made it to her quarters without being noticed, she was wrong. Hakani, the Leader's mate, had seen them both come in. It was evident to Hakani that Adia was trying to move quietly, unseen, keeping to the shadows. She was carrying a full satchel—and had one of the Brothers' females with her, which would have been unusual under any circumstances.

Hakani had been hoping her prayers were answered and Adia had met some untimely accident when she did not return earlier. She had been disheartened to see Adia was still in one piece. Despite her disappointment, her curiosity was piqued by what Adia was up to.

Anyone in their right mind would never do what Hakani did next. But whether Hakani was in her right mind, or had been for some time, was up for debate. Her dislike of Adia was so strong it distorted her thinking.

The Healer's Quarters were sacrosanct. No one would think to enter them without permission and certainly not in the still of the night while the two females slept, defenseless. The Healer's Quarters were to be entered only by the Healer, the Healer's Helper, or at the invitation of either.

Driven by the need to know what Adia had smuggled into her quarters, Hakani entered their living area.

The Healer's Quarters were expansive, with the sleeping area sequestered off to the back, separated from the eating and work areas. She had never been in these quarters before, and she stood in the dark, looking around to get her bearings.

Hakani spied two females resting on sleeping mats with a third on another makeshift arrangement over to the side. She scanned the rest of the area for the satchel Adia had been carrying. She found it next to the work area and realized it was empty when she lifted it.

Fearing she had stayed too long, she turned to leave, but as she did, Hakani saw movement on the sleeping mat next to Adia. She slowly crept back over to the area and bent over the sleeping Healer to see if something there truly had moved or if it was a trick of the dark brought on by her nervousness at what she was doing.

At first, she could not figure out what it was. It

was tiny. It was so still that it almost did not look real. *What has she found now? An orphaned opossum? Or some other wretched creature injured in the woods?*

She gingerly leaned closer, being sure not to lose her balance. Finally, she was close enough to make out what it was.

Her eyes grew wide in disbelief. Her mouth hung open, and she almost gasped out loud but caught herself in time. "*Waschini!*" The word formed in her mind immediately and almost escaped her lips.

Adia, Healer of the People of the High Rocks, Second Rank over the largest tribe of the People known anywhere, had broken one of the Second Laws. Not just broken it, but shattered it completely. She had brought an Outsider into the community. But not only an Outsider, such as a member of an unfamiliar tribe of the Brothers—no, *the worst possible kind*.

Hakani smiled, and her heart beat faster as she pictured her mate's wrath when he learned what Adia had done. He was the Alpha, a male infused with a formidable will, and nothing made him angrier than an affront to his authority. Adia had broken a Second Law, and Hakani understood her mate well enough to know he would take this personally, which would inflame his anger even higher. He was imminently sensitive to the slightest hint of disloyalty, and for someone in Adia's position to break any of the laws would reflect terribly on him as the Leader.

She backed away from the Waschini offspring, praying it did not make a noise and wake either of the two females. *Luckily for me, they are both exhausted from whatever they were up to.* Hakani was not sure which she was going to enjoy more—Adia's punishment at the hands of Khon'Tor, or Khon'Tor's anger and rage at what Adia had done. *Yes, the repercussions are going to be something to relish for a long time.*

Hakani was almost hopping with excitement. She could not wait to tell Khon'Tor, and for Adia's sake, she would make sure to pick the worst moment possible to do so.

Khon'Tor was away, and she just hoped she would not have to wait long.

The Ancients founded the People's laws. The First Laws established the rules for conduct across all the communities of the People. The Second Laws directed the structure of the communities. They detailed the hierarchy of authority, rules of conduct in conflict, and reverence for females and offspring.

The People were slow to change. For generations, they had lived much as they did now, reminded of who they were by the First and Second Laws. It was mostly unheard of that any of the People would violate the laws, because the laws reflected the values of the People as they naturally lived, instead of controlling them with the threat of consequences.

The laws were mostly there to remind the People who they were, and to allow them to connect with the best of themselves. They merely drew a line between what was already part of the People's intrinsic nature, and what was an aberration. The laws had been formed after a period in their history of much struggle, internal and external.

As she made her way back through the tunnel to the Leader's Quarters, though never one to give Adia any quarter, Hakani could not help but marvel a bit at the nerve of someone who would risk such a thing. More than anyone, Adia did this knowing full well she was breaking Sacred Law. Hakani hoped Adia's position as Healer would not mitigate the consequences too much.

She considered how best to let her mate know of the transgression. There were many ways to do it— but one thing Hakani knew for certain; *she* had to be the one to tell him. *I cannot wait too long. I am sure Adia will come forward and tell Khon'Tor herself as soon as she can. Adia is not one to hide from the consequences of her actions.*

Had Hakani not despised Adia so deeply for other reasons, she might even have admired the Healer for that quality.

Adia stirred in her sleep. *Someone was standing over her. Someone who meant her harm. Her heart beat wildly in her chest. She tried to scream, but nothing came out. She could not move; she could not defend herself. There was no one to help her.*

Suddenly, she woke. Her eyes flew open, and she sat up, scanning the room. No one was standing there. She tried to recall who had been leaning over her. She had not been able to make out the face, but the presence had felt like the Leader's mate, Hakani.

She lay back on her sleeping mat to wait for dawn, unable to shake off the dream. Her thoughts turned to Hakani.

If Khon'Tor was difficult to deal with as the People's Leader, his mate ran a close second. Hakani was nowhere near as complex as her mate Khon'Tor; she was a female driven purely by ambition. As Leader's mate, she occupied the Third Rank and obviously enjoyed her position, though it seemed to eat at her that the Healer's rank fell above her own.

There was more to the tension between them than that, but what, not even Adia's seventh sense had revealed to her. She registered it as jealousy on Hakani's part, though she could not understand the source of it. Adia had no interest in the Leader as a mate if that was what Hakani thought. And even if Adia were not forbidden to take a mate, Khon'Tor would never be her choice.

It was not that he was not attractive. Given the chance, there was probably not a female alive who would not stare at him shamelessly. He was huge of stature, broad-chested, with well-developed muscular lines, and the striking silver streak running across his crown made him stand out even more. Considering physical attributes alone, he was extraordinary. But his heart was cold, and he led from an iron will—and there was nothing Adia valued more than heart. And there was nothing of which she was warier than a powerful will disconnected from the guidance of the heart.

Had she even had the right to mate, her choice would never be the Alpha male Khon'Tor, no matter how commanding his presence.

CHAPTER 4

As soon as there was light to see by, while Arina nursed him, Adia immediately got to work setting up a nesting area for the Outsider. *Thank goodness we are at the far end of Kthama. He is going to have to be kept here for now.*

While Adia was making a place for him to sleep by moving some items out of one of the storage alcoves, Nadiwani awoke and started her usual litany of questions in any new situation.

"Do you think it goes through the same cycles as ours? Infancy, Youth, Prime-of-Life, Middle-Age, Senior, Twilight, and then finally, Return to the Great Spirit?"

Taking a break from rearranging the quarters, Adia looked up to answer Nadiwani.

"I do think so, because of the two adults who were murdered where I found him. In the way they were formed, they looked similar to our offspring-bearing age. All the other creatures go through the stages; I do not know why they would be exempt."

Adia noticed again how quiet the offspring was. *Considering what it's been through, I would think it should be more agitated. Oh no, what if it is sick? What if that is why it was so quiet on the journey here? What if I have not only committed a serious transgression against my people by bringing in an Outsider—what if I brought some contagion in with it?*

Adia joined Nadiwani over by the offspring. She lifted it up and inspected it, letting it dangle in front of her. It was incredibly light, and she turned it around, examining its little feet, its toes, its arms, and its fingers.

If this is what the Waschini are like, how could they be such a threat to the People? This is the frailest, most fragile thing I have ever seen.

"Look at it, Nadiwani. It is incredibly pale and has very little hair covering. Its only redeeming quality is that it is so utterly helpless and pathetic—that, and those bright sky-blue eyes."

She noticed it felt a little cool to the touch, but was not surprised because it had very little natural protection from the elements. All the while she was handling the offspring, it wore the same stupid grin on its face, smiling up at her with those impossibly bright eyes.

Oh, and it stank. This seemed to be a standard quality with the Waschini, from what everyone said of them. And it made their presence easy enough to detect. They were very loud in their speech. They did not know how to move quietly through the forest and made all types of clamor. They left destruction behind them everywhere they went, whacking away at the trees and undergrowth instead of moving branches and bending saplings out of their way. They left behind cast-offs and waste. Worst of all, they relieved themselves everywhere. With the highly tuned senses of the People, it was not hard to know when a Waschini had passed through an area, even if only briefly. Luckily, their presence was a rare occurrence.

For a moment, Adia wondered if it was not sick but was somehow addle-minded. *How could something this calm and agreeable grow into a monster? Surely this cooing, ridiculously happy, stinky thing would be the exception to the rule.*

Adia sat the offspring down on a bed of reeds. Turning to Nadiwani, she said, "We need to name this offspring. And we need to arrange for a wet nurse here. And for heaven's sake, we need to *clean it up.*"

Nadiwani chuckled and said, "I already thought of that. It certainly needs a bath. And it will need to nurse frequently," she said, signing the word for 'be at breast'.

Adia scrunched her face up at the thought that she could not expect Arina to stay here indefinitely. The longer this continued, the more she realized she had not worked it through.

There are new mothers with more than enough milk to spare for him. But how in the world am I going to convince any one of them to let this repulsive creature latch on? After all, none of them had heard any redeeming stories about the Waschini. Adia feared it would take all her powers of persuasion to pull this off. It was different for Arina; there was not that much difference physically between the Brothers and the Waschini.

Albeit that some of their differences were great, there were basic structural similarities between the People and the Waschini. Though it was frail now, she was sure it would survive under their care. She almost added the words 'and grow strong', but abandoned the thought immediately. *Whatever this offspring will be, strength and vigor will not be any of its attributes*, she thought—at least not by the People's standards.

Both the males and females of the tribe respected and looked up to Adia. They knew the character of her father, the previous Leader of the neighboring People of the Deep Valley. They recognized her exceptional skills as a Healer and her deep connection to the Great Mother through the strength of the seventh sense that circulated through her core. She knew she had their favor and their support. *But how far can that favor be stretched? Surely there is a breaking point of any loyalty.*

Even beyond the overwhelming general goodwill toward her among both genders, the females of the community had an even stronger connection to her. Adia's position as Second Rank gave voice to females' issues, different from those of the males. Though females of the People were cherished as givers of life and were always to be treated with respect, it comforted them to have someone in a leadership position to speak from their female platform.

Many of the females felt sorry for the restrictions which forbade the Healer to mate and have offspring of her own. The females of the People were natural mothers. They cared deeply for their offspring and took delight in raising and teaching them. Despite whatever glories and honor there were to being a Healer, they knew Adia was missing out on one of a female's greatest pleasures.

Because of their critical role, Healers were forbidden by the Second Laws to be paired or produce offspring. The threat of the loss of a Healer through complications while carrying and delivering an offspring presented too great a risk. Without a mate or offspring, Healers were committed solely to the welfare of the People. And because they did not have a direct family of their own, their judgment was considered to be more impartial than that of the Leader, who was required to mate and reproduce.

Adia ran through a mental list of the females closest to her in the community. She was seeking those who would be an advocate for her in convincing one of the nursing mothers to help. She knew she would be asking them to join her in this treasonous act. Perhaps even share in punishment down the road. Well, perhaps not treasonous but certainly a crime, as it violated the Second Laws: No Contact With Outsiders.

Though the First Laws had never been modified, as time passed, one additional law had been added: Never Without Consent.

In the history of the People, there had been few violations of either the First or Second Laws. The fact that the Ancients had to add a law banning the nonconsensual mating of a female was a dark stain on the history of the People. Females were revered as givers of life, and to mate with one against her will was anathema. Adia hoped this creature's mother had passed before the men who killed both his parents had violated her.

She pursed her lips as she went through the candidates from whom she could ask for help.

While Adia was lost in these thoughts, Nadiwani started trying to clean up the offspring.

"It needs a name," she said when she finally caught Adia's eye.

"Well, yes, it does. I guess we cannot continue to call it the Outsider, or the Waschini," agreed Adia. Neither of these terms was complementary and certainly did not set a tone for acceptance of the tiny creature.

She immediately thought of Oh'Mah, which meant Master of the Forest. But, as much as she liked the name, she knew it would only fuel Khon'Tor's ire.

Adia became silent, suddenly remembering something her father told her long, long ago; something she had forgotten about until now.

"He will be called Oh'Dar," she said.

"I have not heard that name before. Did you make it up?" asked Nadiwani.

"No. It is from a story my father told me once," she said quietly.

Since the easiest problem to fix was to clean Oh'Dar up, they took to solving that one first. What they needed was a body of water sufficient to wash the stench off the offspring, and they had nothing of that volume at hand. They dared not use the females' bathing area for fear of discovery.

Almost simultaneously both said, "Gnoaii!"

The Mother Stream, which snaked through the lowest level of Kthama, was their most valued resource. Not only did it bring fresh water and oxygen directly into their underground living space, but they had also been able to repurpose parts of it. In places, the Mother Stream split off into other smaller streams, some of which were modified long ago by the People for their specific purposes. Parts of the Mother Stream had been diverted into smaller grottos or enclosed caves, creating several small indoor ponds. Channels similar to the one which brought light into Adia's quarters enabled moss and other ground covers to grow. At the end of Fall, the People stocked the one called the Gnoaii with fish from the outside rivers and streams.

The Gnoaii was used to winter-over, to keep a food supply of fish available for potential lean stretches. Not yet stocked, the clear waters still trickled slowly through the shallow pool—it was perfect for the task at hand, and the water would be refreshed by the time it was needed.

'This is good timing, Nadiwani. Most of the community is already going about their business and will be outside. We should be able to sneak little Oh'Dar down to the Gnoaii without being spotted."

"Well, let's hope his good nature stands up to this."

Being careful not to be seen—though few visited during the warmer months—they sneaked Oh'Dar to the Gnoaii. Nadiwani dipped the offspring into the shallowest, warmest part of the quiet waters, and though his blue eyes widened, he only squirmed a little, pulling his toes up at first. The People were not averse to water, but they did not take to it the way this one did, that was certain.

After they had him cleaned up and wrapped in a warm covering, they returned to their quarters. Nadiwani added more wrappings to make sure he did not catch a chill. Being underground, the living areas of the caves were temperate—cooler than the outside temperatures in summer, and warmer in winter months.

That challenge met, Adia resigned herself to face the problem of finding one of their own females to take over nursing Oh'Dar. She knew that in her position of Second Rank, she could order one of the females to accept the offspring. *That would be the way Khon'Tor would handle it, that's for sure.* But using her authority to enforce her will was never Adia's way.

She realized she needed a stepped approach, rather than a direct one—like throwing a pebble in a body of water and letting the ripples expand. She thought of the females who were closest to her, her strongest supporters; females who themselves were in a position of influence within the community.

Adia also realized this meeting with the females could go very wrong. *If they have the same first reaction as Nadiwani, I might never get their support. I need to set the stage to convey to them the importance and reverence of this event.*

"Nadiwani, please go and find Donoma, Lomasi, Mapiya, and Haiwee and bring them here," she said.

"Donoma and Haiwee will probably be out in the preparation area. I do not know about Lomasi and Mapiya. But until you have all four gathered, do not bring any of them here. I want to address them together, at the same time," Adia directed.

Nadiwani shook her head a couple of times. "Here?" she asked. "Here in the Healer's Quarters?"

It was an unprecedented move because of the sanctity of the Healer's Quarters.

"I mean," Nadiwani stammered, "It's never been done before, bringing anyone here from the community."

"Yes, here," nodded Adia. "Here to my quarters."

Nadiwani shook her head again but did as Adia said. After all, Adia had just brought one of the Brothers there.

She had no trouble rounding up the first two, directing them to wait in the Great Chamber until she had the others collected. Finally, having found all four females, she asked them to come with her and not to ask any questions. The females looked at each other, acknowledging the unprecedented honor of being called by Nadiwani.

The Helper led them from the Great Chamber through the expansive stone tunnels to Adia's quarters. She turned back to check and saw the females were not following her. They had stopped at the entrance of the tunnel that led to the Healer's Quarters. Nadiwani went back to them and again asked that they come with her. The first in line, Mapiya, looked back at the others as if checking they had all understood the same thing. Finally, Nadiwani beckoned them by swooping her hand into the tunnel to simulate their entering, and they followed her through the opening.

Once inside, the females looked around furtively. Nadiwani imagined their curiosity must be overwhelming—after all, the chances of them ever being here again was virtually non-existent—once in a lifetime was even outside their wildest imaginings.

While waiting, Adia had prepared for the females' arrival. She placed Oh'Dar out of sight, praying he would continue to be quiet. She had not prepared a speech but instead spent the time in meditation, counting on her connection to the Great Mother to guide her in what to say.

Everything within her still said that Oh'Dar had a role to play, an important role, in the future of her people—maybe even that of the Brothers also. Though she had ultimately saved him based on an overriding motherly instinct, the sense of his importance had reinforced her decision to rescue the offspring and bring him here.

Standing, Adia motioned them to please sit in front of her and signed to Nadiwani and Arina of the Brothers to stand beside her.

Adia was not the tallest female in the community, but she was of above-average stature. Now that the four visitors were all sitting, she realized she was towering over them—not the atmosphere of collaboration she wished to foster for this meeting.

Adia lowered herself to the ground, sitting cross-legged in front of the females, not more than five feet away. She reached up to Nadiwani and Arina and pulled them down to sit next to her—the three of them now facing the other females. Adia sat close enough to the four to bring them into her personal space. There was enormous goodwill among this group of four females, but none of them was on the familiar standing with Adia that Nadiwani was. The fact that the Healer and Healer's Helper were including the visitors in their inner circle—at least for the moment—was meant to demonstrate that Adia was placing great confidence in them.

It was a good thing Adia started to speak shortly after that, as the females seemed no longer able to contain their excitement. She continued in Handspeak, first introducing Arina.

Handspeak was a graceful language that the People used at will and interchangeably with spoken words. It was particularly useful on hunting parties when speech was the enemy of stealth, and any sound could alert the prey. It was also frequently used during the early and late periods of the day when they did not want to disturb others. Lastly, it was the first language taught to their offspring, as motor skills preceded the development of verbal skills. Mothers and caretakers had discovered they could communicate with their offspring through Handspeak long before the offspring mastered the spoken language. But to use it in the quarters here, when there was no real need to keep the silence, lent a formality to her message.

"I know you are wondering why you are here. I know that on some level, you are aware something important is about to take place—for me individually, and for the People as a whole. I know you have faith in me as your Healer. I hope I have always demonstrated to you by my actions that I have only the best interests of our people at heart. My father passed on to me the love he had for all the People, and it runs through my veins now."

Adia paused for a moment, stopping short of asking them to trust her based on their esteem for her renowned father. It would have been an easy move, but she felt they might perceive it as a critical reflection on their Leader, Khon'Tor, and even more so with him away. *No, Khon'Tor and I may have our differences, but he is still the Leader. I will not do anything to discredit his authority. Well, if this one small violation of the Second Laws by bringing the Waschini offspring here does not count.*

She continued, "Long ago the Ancients foretold that great challenges would come to the People in the far times. So far, we have lived in peace with our neighbors the Brothers, and the multitude of forest souls with whom we share this world. We have enjoyed generation after generation of freedom and protection, not only in raising our young but also in sharing our joys. That is not to say there have not been trials, but the challenges we have faced individually and collectively as a People are nothing compared to the times to come; times that will test our resolve and our commitment to our culture, to the Brothers, and to each other," she signed.

The females never took their eyes off her. The air in the room was still charged but changing, no longer filled with anticipation but with a sense of reverence.

"Each of you is also connected to the Great

Mother through the seventh sense, so you already know there can be deep-running currents which do not ripple the surface. And often only the passage of time and unfolding of events will reveal the hidden deeper truths."

Adia had lost all feelings of concern by now. She was in the flow of her connection with the Great Mother, and the words spilled effortlessly from her hands. She had surrendered to what would be, trusting that a great power was in control of Oh'Dar's destiny as well as her own, and the role they would play together in the future of her people.

Adia took a deep breath before continuing, maintaining eye contact with the group, but softening her gaze. Her hands moved fluidly, but slower now.

"I have committed a grievous sin against the laws of the People. I do not involve you in this sin. It was mine alone, and I accept full responsibility for it, just as I will accept the consequences of my actions," she continued.

The four females exchanged quick sideways glances with each other.

Adia stood up, went to a corner of the room, and came back carrying the offspring.

She stood before them holding Oh'Dar, his tiny, frail body cradled in her arms. The females did not make a sound. They looked at the offspring, taking in the light fuzz on the top of his head, the tiny arms, the tinier fingers. Just as she had not, Adia was confident they had never seen a more fragile creature in their lives. Then he turned his head and looked at them with those brilliant blue eyes, at the same time making a little bubbly cooing noise.

For a moment, nothing was said. Not a hand moved. All eyes were on the Waschini offspring in front of them. Almost all the People had heard stories of the White Men—of their cruelty and their cowardice. Some of them knew only that Whites existed. Either way, the enormity of Adia's act was unprecedented.

Slowly, Mapiya stood up and approached Adia. She put her hand out slowly, gently, and gingerly placed it on top of the offspring's head. She looked up at Adia and with her other hand asked,

"How can we help you?"

With that, the others also stood and joined them. By now, Nadiwani was in tears. Tears also welled in Adia's eyes. She felt the connection between all of them, and with the Great Mother, deepen and quicken. At that moment, she knew they were all bonded together in this – no matter what might come.

Understanding having been established, Adia sat back down, now with Oh'Dar in her lap. The other females followed her lead and sat around her in a semi-circle. Under different circumstances, if an offspring were introduced, there would have been light-hearted chatter about names and training, and the offspring would have been passed around to be cooed over, with many words of congratulations for the new mother. But this was a solemn event with no place for levity or empty chatter.

It was as if no one wanted to break the mood. Finally, the oldest of the four females, Mapiya, spoke up. "Arina cannot stay with us forever. He needs a wet nurse from the People." It was a statement, not a question. Adia and Nadiwani both nodded. The older female raised her hand as if to say, "*No problem, it is done.*"

Based on what had just taken place between them, Adia had no doubts that Mapiya would come through in producing someone to nurse the offspring; though it would be no small feat to find someone built small enough for this tiny mouth to latch onto.

At that point, Nadiwani spoke up and took over the conversation, speaking to the group about the offspring's needs for food, clothing, and care. Adia took the opportunity to get up and place Oh'Dar back in his protected area where he could stay warm.

She turned back to look at the females, her new inner circle, all talking at the same time, excited and energized. The barrier had been cracked; he was no longer so much a Waschini as he was simply an offspring.

Several days passed. Khon'Tor had not yet returned and had sent no word that he was on his way. Adia used the time to her advantage, strengthening the connection between her and the other females, arranging logistics for the care of Oh'Dar.

True to her word, Mapiya had found a wet nurse for him.

"This is Pakuna. You remember her; she was paired three years ago," said Mapiya. To her credit, the young female did not flinch when she saw the offspring. She took him in her arms and helped him latch on. Pakuna had produced her first offspring not very many days before. New mothers generally had more than enough milk for several offspring, and as tiny as Oh'Dar was, she would hardly notice his draw on her supply.

Adia reflected on this first step. True, it was only a small group of females—but they were influential in the rest of the community. She believed she had chosen well, though the real test would occur when the Leader returned and it was time for Adia to face the consequences of her actions.

CHAPTER 5

The mighty Khon'Tor was silent as he returned from his trip. He had traveled easily four days on foot to meet with the High Council. Almost every one of the High Council members had been there. It had been a special meeting, called to address growing concerns about the Outsiders and their encroachment on both the People's and the Brothers' territory. But his silence was not from physical fatigue; the trip there and back was nothing for a male of his strength and build. He could easily have covered three times the distance and not been taxed; it was the mental strain that had drained his reserves.

The High Council members had shared more stories of the White Man's cruelty and ignorance. The Waschini demonstrated abject disregard for the gifts of the Great Spirit. They showed no consideration to using only what they needed and to leave the rest to fulfill its role in the natural order. They had no reverence for the forest creatures, no respect for the value of animals' lives. They hunted creatures to extinction.

The High Council members questioned whether the Waschini possessed a soul; they seemed cruel and heartless, showing no mercy and giving no quarter. Of this, they all agreed; the coming of the Outsiders promised nothing good for the Brothers or the People.

The People had always moved freely throughout the vast expanse of their land. They had no fear of the forest, the rivers, the animals, or any of the other tribes. They had respect for and lived in harmony with the Brothers. But the Outsiders seemed to have no laws, no conscience, no heart to which to appeal. They seemed to lack an internal stop, which meant any limit to their destructive power had to be forced on them externally.

Neither the People nor the Brothers were afraid of conflict. It was never their first solution, however. They preferred to live in peace. Whether they were able to defend themselves and their communities was not the point. But they had learned that once conflict started it only escalated. If there was no will to avoid the conflict in the first place, there was very little chance of achieving the greater task of stopping it. And this meant that on all sides everybody—community, family, friends, mates, offspring, resources—ultimately lost.

The High Council had spent days discussing the ancient concept of Wrak-Ayya. The fall of Wrak-Ayya would make the lives of all much harder.

There were tales that in the oldest of days the Ancients had all possessed the extra sense—the males as well as the females. The ancient stories handed down told of the males' ability being stripped from them as punishment by the Great Spirit, though the details were murky as to what their crime had been. But in those times, whether the vision came to the females only, or to all the People, they foresaw that changes would come to their communities many generations in the future. Wrak-Ayya, the Age of Shadows would usher in changes which would create hardship for everyone. Though the warning of the Age of Shadows had been given by the Ancients, the details had not. They had not foreseen the particulars of when or why the shadow of Wrak-Ayya might descend. Or, if they had, these were not shared outside of a select few. It would not be the first time information had been withheld from all but a small, protective circle.

In preparation, the High Council members had roughed out four levels of Wrak-Ayya. These levels provided a stepped system, with the intent to contain hardships at as low a level as possible. In each of their hearts, the High Council Leaders hoped never to have to evoke any of the levels—let alone the higher, most restrictive ones.

Before they adjourned, they had agreed they

should share these decisions about Wrak-Ayya with their communities at the time each Leader deemed most appropriate. For those in the outer regions, the communities of the Far Flats, the Great Pines and High Red Rocks, the time to invoke Wrak-Ayya was not close at hand—might not come for centuries still. Khon'Tor was afraid his people, the People of the High Rocks, might not be as fortunate.

Khon'Tor turned their situation over in his mind with each step of his return. He knew the path well, so he walked on, deep in thought, his heavy footfalls and slumped shoulders reflecting the burden he was carrying.

Ogima Adoeete, Chief of the Brothers, and their Second Chief, Is'Taqa, walked with him in silence. Since their territories bordered each other, they often traveled to and from the High Council meetings together. Having made most of the journey along the underground passage bordering the Mother Stream, Ogima Adoeete had asked that they surface and cover the rest of the way above ground. The Brothers were not as accustomed to being underground as the People.

Were it not for his High Protector Acaraho, Khon'Tor would have borne all the weight of his responsibilities as Leader alone. He could, and would, seek the counsel of the Healer and of his mate, Hakani, who were respectively second and third in command. There was not, however, an easy alliance between the three. Some level of tension, even bordering on animosity, was always present. He understood it well enough from his side—but as a male, he did not have the females' seventh sense so he could not read the reason for his mate's dislike of the Healer.

Whatever conflict had taken place between Hakani and Adia, Hakani had never confided in him. He only knew his mate bristled when Adia spoke and that her eyes followed the Healer with a dark, low-burning glare.

The sun had set, and the moon was high in the sky by the time the three neared the edge of the People's cave. It had been a long trip. Khon'Tor had slowed his pace to meet Ogima Adoeete's, and in turn, Ogima Adoeete had increased his. Though Khon'Tor was not physically tired, he knew Ogima Adoeete surely had to be close to exhaustion. As well as being far smaller, as all the Brothers were, the Chief was considerably older and in less ideal physical condition. Khon'Tor could easily have carried the Chief, but they were equals, and Ogima Adoeete would never have put Khon'Tor in a position of subservience. Khon'Tor, his own Leader's Staff in his hand, noticed Ogima Adoeete used his Chief's Staff as support for quite a bit of the trip.

"Ogima Adoeete," he addressed the Chief. "Your trail is long yet. Come in and let us keep you and

Is'Taqa for the night. It might also be beneficial for us to speak together tomorrow before you return to your people."

To Khon'Tor's surprise, Ogima Adoeete nodded, taking him up on his offer for a night's place of rest.

The moment the three walked into the Great Entrance, the guards on duty and a small collection of community members jumped up and ran over to greet them. Khon'Tor explained that the High Chief and his Second would be staying with the People for the night, and they quickly went about setting up hospitality. Ordinarily, Acaraho, Khon'Tor's High Protector, would take care of such matters, but he was not on duty at present.

It had been generations since the People were engaged in physical battle. But the People learned from history. Though there might not be a present need for an organized defense, having acknowledged roles for protection was still wise. There were defined roles of watcher and guard, all under the command of the People's High Protector, Acaraho. However, the long periods of peace allowed these males often to turn their focus to organized hunting parties, scouting expeditions, and maintenance of the caves and structures. Once his guests were taken care of, Khon'Tor made the long trek through the curved stone tunnels to his quarters. He released a sigh of relief that Hakani was still asleep. It was just as well, as he only wanted peace, and theirs had turned into an uneasy union over time.

Khon'Tor looked at Hakani resting and reflected on how he had chosen her to be his mate.

Above all the ranks within the community, including the Leader himself, was the High Council, a combination of Leaders and Chiefs from the tribes in the area who came together to discuss matters of mutual concern. Unless specifically called to settle a dispute within a community, the High Council seldom met with the general population, with one exception. These meetings were a time of coming together, reunification, and pairing—the Ashwea Awhidi.

At the times of Ashwea Awhidi, the High Council shared information of general interest, granted requests for specific pairings by couples who felt they were called to be paired, and made the Council's pairing announcements. Any other high-level business affecting that community would also be conducted then. At the end, the Leader of the community was given the platform to make any summary comments or announcements to his people.

All pairings were planned and approved by the High Council, except those of the Leaders. In the ancient days, this was not the case; however, the dwindling population of the People mandated that new blood had to be brought into the communities to ensure the health of the generations to come.

They had learned that over time, breeding that was too close weakened the future generations.

Only Kthama could hold such a large gathering, so members from neighboring communities traveled there. Those who could used the pathway that ran parallel to the Mother Stream, below in the underground world of the People.

Benches of large rock slabs and boulders were brought in for seating on those occasions where bigger numbers gathered. The ground at the highest end of the chamber had been intentionally raised so the People attending could see the High Council members and speakers more easily. Females and offspring took time bringing in flowers and other adornments to add to the festive atmosphere; others spent time beforehand in preparatory meditation, raising the energy in the chamber as high as possible.

As Leader of his people, not being under the jurisdiction of the High Council in approval of a pairing, Khon'Tor had the right to choose his own mate. He knew the importance of a good match and had taken his time in making his selection. He had met the maidens from the nearby communities, but none of them had caught or held his eye for long— Except one.

The truth was, he could not get his mind off her. He had been watching her, studying her, every chance he had. He had seen her when he had traveled to a neighboring community to meet with its

Leaders because they shared similar challenges in their underground living.

She was exactly what he wanted in every regard; strong, beautiful, with the deepest large dark brown eyes, intelligent, and high spirited enough to spark and keep his interest. The fact that she came from a respected line herself was a tremendous attribute and could only add to his influence; a point not at all lost on one as ambitious as Khon'Tor. Lastly, he was confident she would give him many fine offspring from which the next Leader would be selected.

Khon'Tor was excited to announce his selection. Traditionally, the maiden concerned had no idea she had been chosen. It was a great honor to be picked as the Leader's mate, and as it was known that such an announcement was coming from the great Khon'Tor himself, the anticipation in the room was practically crackling.

The High Council Overseer made his announcements, approved two self-directed pairings, and had one other matter to decide before Khon'Tor could take the floor. He knew exactly where she was standing in the crowd. At every chance, he let his eyes linger over her figure, following every curve and imagining the time when he could finally run his hands over them—and more.

His heart was racing as the time approached. He hoped no one was aware of his excitement. To Khon'-Tor, it was unseemly for a Leader to be so undone by a female—even more for a male with as much pride as he had.

Though he knew he should be paying more attention to the other business, as this was a critical time for his people, Khon'Tor's mind wandered to his favorite anticipations; her reaction when he revealed her name, and the overwhelming support from the People at the wisdom of his choice. Lastly, and which he probably spent too much time imagining, his anticipation of the shared intimacies between them that would soon follow. Khon'Tor was a robust male, and he had been waiting to be paired for what felt like a very long time.

Only one more piece of business stood between him and his taking the stage. In reality, this was as important a turning point for his people as for him, though not as personal. It was time to announce the new Healer of the People of the High Rocks.

A terrible tragedy had befallen the previous Healer. With her loss, the Healer's Helper had taken over all primary responsibilities. She was a talented chemist, well versed in the herbs and plants in their area, and their uses. She was good-natured and amiable, and Khon'Tor had no qualms about her being selected as the next Healer, second in command under him. He was confident Nadiwani would not present a challenge to his authority because he could easily assert his domination over her, which would give him almost full control of the People. This piece of business was just a formality, just something standing between his claim and his ultimate enjoyment of *her*.

His mind's wanderings were abruptly ended when he heard the High Council spokesman call her name. His head snapped up, and he looked around, confused. He spotted her moving forward to the platform.

What is going on?

Grateful that all eyes were on her, he took a moment to regain his control. Though his mind and heart were racing, with effort, he controlled his body language so as not to betray his confusion.

He watched her step gracefully onto the platform and stand next to the Council spokesman, who took her hand and raised it in his own. At that moment, a spontaneous response of approval arose from the crowd, and shock finally cleared the fog from Khon'-Tor's mind.

The High Council had chosen *her* as the Healer for *his* people. He had been so confident that Nadi-wani, the Healer's Helper, would be selected as the next Healer. That another might be chosen had never occurred to him, least of all that they would choose *her*. He had not considered that she could be snatched from him before he even had a chance to claim her, but here it was; she had been chosen as the next Healer. Adia was now lost to him forever.

Healers were not established by lineage but were selected based on attributes such as character, honor, compassion, empathy, intelligence, and most importantly, the strength of her connection to the Great Mother. In fact, many present were thinking it was a shame Adia's lineage would end with her—because Healers could not mate. It was a tremendous loss to the People that there would be no part of her passed on through her bloodline to enrich the community.

Khon'Tor could not move. *She is now Second Rank to my First. I will have to work side by side with her. She will be part of Kthama now. I will have to see her every day, knowing I can never have her. Ever.*

The High Council Overseer was looking directly at Khon'Tor, waiting for him to approach the platform. The word had already leaked out that he had made his selection for a mate.

I cannot back down now. If I do, enough of them will work it out. And what if she works it out? Even worse.

If he did not think quickly, he risked losing face among his people, and frankly, he would rather be dead than suffer that. He remembered the Overseer trying to speak with him earlier; was this what he had been going to say—that they had selected Adia as Healer to his people?

After the commotion had quieted and Adia had stepped down and taken her place back among the crowd, the High Council Overseer nodded to Khon'Tor to approach. His thoughts were in turmoil; he had not considered a second choice. He walked slowly, methodically placing his feet one after the other. He had only seconds to make a decision that would follow him at the most intimate level for the rest of his life. He quickly reviewed the parade of maidens from the other communities. He could remember only one, a female with no particularly stand-out qualities but who seemed to be good-natured, even-tempered, and of good, healthy stock. Since he had lost the one he truly desired, at that moment it did not seem to matter who he now chose.

He had only a fraction of time to look out over the crowd before speaking. He saw the other maiden there and breathed a sigh of relief that she was at least in attendance. Khon'Tor gritted his teeth, pushing down his anger at himself for not seeing this possible outcome. He made a few opening statements and then announced his choice, "Hakani of the People of the Little River."

The People all looked around to see who this female was, the choice of their Leader. It took them a moment to find her in the crowd.

Hakani looked up toward the front at hearing her name. She froze. *Khon'Tor has chosen me? I did not know he favored me. I never noticed him giving me a second look.*

She was taken aback, and it took a moment for it to hit her. She had been chosen by the Leader to be his mate. *I will be Third Rank of the largest community of the People in all the known regions. I will be the one he turns to, the great Khon'Tor, for counsel, support, comfort. I will be the mother of the next Leader of the High Rocks.*

Yes, she would have to leave her own community, and she felt a pang of loss for the day-to-day contact with her family and the comfort it brought; but this was a high honor—an opportunity to be grabbed and ridden for all it was worth.

Hakani collected herself and realized all eyes were on her. She took her time going up to the platform, relishing the attention and the honor. When she stood beside him, now the intended mate of Khon'Tor, Leader of the People of the High Rocks, she could not believe her luck and good fortune.

The two stood next to each other, while the second round of excited commotion moved through the crowd.

Khon'Tor took a moment to deal with his inner turmoil, trying to resign himself to a lifetime with this female of whom he knew very little, and reeling over the loss of his beautiful Adia. He spotted her in the crowd, watching him being paired with another, not knowing she had slipped from his fingers at the last moment due to his arrogance and unpreparedness.

This is inexcusable. I am Khon'Tor of the High Rocks. It is my duty to be prepared for all outcomes. I should have made time for the Overseer. Perhaps I could have changed their decision, and she would be mine now instead of lost to me forever.

And at that moment, he started to shift his disappointment and grief to something else. At that moment, unable to bear his self-recrimination for not having foreseen this possibility, and unable to handle the loss of everything he had imagined with

Adia as his mate, he began to turn all this muddled churning mass of pain into something else, something easier to live with. Something he felt to be more becoming of a great Leader.

It is beneath me to let a female get to me so strongly. Adia must never know she was the one I wanted at my side, that she was my First Choice. She is just a female, he told himself. *One is as good as another.* He did not believe this lie, but right now, he needed the lie more than he needed the truth.

Using all his will, Khon'Tor took his longing and desire for Adia and started distorting it into something easier to live with—he began to resent the new Healer as deeply as he had wanted her.

Hakani and Khon'Tor could not be further apart in their reactions to this turn of events. Khon'Tor was at one of the lowest points of his life. He looked at Hakani standing next to him, beaming with pride at being chosen. He consoled himself that at least this was an even-tempered female; she would be easy to manage. She was healthy and of sturdy build. She did not possess the physical beauty Adia did, but she was pleasant enough. Most importantly, she would give him the offspring he needed. Leadership could only be passed to a blood heir.

Khon'Tor and Hakani had one thing in common; neither of them could have been more wrong about what their relationship would bring.

Khon'Tor left his painful reminiscing and again looked down at his sleeping mate. *She turned out to be nothing of what I assessed her to be. She is not even-tempered. She is not wise, though she is clever. She was once a help to me in the mechanics of our union but nothing more. She is more a detriment than anything. Her heart is filled with discontent and resentment—even hatred. I do not even know the reason for her vile disposition toward me.*

He had done his best to hide his disappointment at losing Adia. Just as he had vowed Adia would never know she was his First Choice, Hakani would never know she was *not* his First Choice and had been selected by default in a moment of immeasurable pressure—thrust upon him by his own failings.

All in all, it was worse than an unsatisfactory union. It was a debilitating one. In the beginning, he had taken the time to try and develop a satisfying relationship. He was gentle with her, putting her pleasure before his. He knew it was the male's responsibility to make the female come to him. But despite his attentions and patience, after a while she suddenly stopped responding to him at all, ignoring his signs that he wanted her. And on top of all that, she had not yet borne him any offspring. Based on the infrequency and dissatisfaction of their matings, he feared she never would. They were young, and the Leader had time, but he did not have forever.

Hakani awoke to the presence of her mate sleeping beside her. Her initial feeling of disappointment that he was back was immediately replaced with recollection of the night before, and anticipation of the turmoil about to ensue. It was all she could do not to wake him and tell him immediately what Adia had done, but she didn't, of course. She wanted his reaction and Adia's rebuke to be as public and as much of a shock as possible.

If Hakani had any remorse or a tweak of conscience at what she was planning, it was beyond her awareness. In her mind, they both deserved it— and more.

Hakani rose and tended to the tasks of the day, waiting for Khon'Tor to awake. She did not try to move quietly; she was anxious for the day's events to unfold. Finally, her noisy preparations caused him to stir.

"Welcome back," said Hakani. "How was the Council meeting?"

Khon'Tor propped himself up on one elbow and frowned at her. He was not sure why Hakani was even speaking to him, as they usually ignored each other and went about their own business.

"There is much I have to share, Hakani. Great challenges are facing our people. I will be calling a general meeting this afternoon. Ogima Adoeete stayed and rested here with us last night, and I want to speak with him beforehand. I might even ask him to attend the meeting with us as a show of the continued cooperation between our tribes," he told her.

It was the longest conversation they'd had in some time. Hakani smiled to herself on getting the information she needed. *With Khon'Tor calling a general assembly, everyone in the community will be present. Whatever his announcement to the People, it will have to wait. This is my chance to deal Adia a blow from which she will never recover.*

This was her opportunity, and she intended to use it to her fullest advantage.

Back in her quarters, Adia had not heard that Khon'Tor had returned, but she had felt it. The minute he stepped into the Great Entrance, she was aware he was back. As a result, she spent a fitful night. However, she had been glad for the opportunity of a few days' preparation before his return. The support of the circle of females she had assembled, and the fact that a wet nurse from their community would be able to provide the essential nourishment Oh'Dar needed, had gone a long way toward equipping her to deal with what was coming.

It did not take long for word of his return to spread. Khon'Tor had set the general assembly for just after high sun. Ogima Adoeete and Is'Taqa would continue their journey to their people after the meeting. The relationship between the Brothers and the People was a comfort to both tribes, and Khon'Tor welcomed the opportunity to demonstrate the continued alliance by their attendance, especially knowing the hardships they might all face in coming times.

Because the leadership of the People was shared, Khon'Tor felt obligated to invite Adia and Hakani to his meeting with Ogima Adoeete the High Chief and Is'Taqa, his Second. In addition to being Second Chief, Is'Taqa was the brother of their Medicine Woman, Ithua; the one to whom Adia had been on her way to deliver the Goldenseal roots.

Khon'Tor felt he needed to share with them what he was going to tell the People. Once Ogima Adoeete agreed they should meet that morning, Khon'Tor had word sent for the Healer.

He hoped Hakani could control her dislike of Adia today. As it was, he was taxed almost to his limits with what was at hand.

Khon'Tor, Ogima Adoeete, Is'Taqa, Hakani, and Adia sat together in a private area set aside for just such purposes. There were several located throughout the corridors, almost all on the first level. Of varying sizes, their cool rock walls lent themselves well to the hosting of meetings. With no openings other than the doorway, words were muffled from the outside, and Handspeak could not be seen.

Khon'Tor went meticulously over the contents of the High Council meeting. The concerns over the coming of the Waschini to their lands, reports of their cruelty and viciousness, their disregard for the resources of the Great Spirit, the fact that they seemed to have no internal limit to control their drives. Ogima Adoeete and Is'Taqa concurred. Khon'Tor dismissed the group, now having told them first what he would tell the People that afternoon.

As Adia listened to Khon'Tor, her earlier peace about coming forward started to dissipate. She wondered if there could be a worse time to have broken one of the Sacred Laws. And to have it be a Waschini offspring she had brought in—

Perhaps I should tell this to Khon'Tor privately. Oh, but word will spread like wildfire through our people. Better to have it all out at once in front of everyone than to have only pieces of it circulate as gossip.

It was not a mistake. Had the river not been too high, I would never have taken the longer route and discovered the offspring. He would have died with his parents, though much more slowly and horribly. Adia reconfirmed to herself her belief that the currents of the stream of life were divinely guided, and decided that whatever may happen, somehow it would work together for good in the end. She just hoped she would live long enough to see it.

While they were all listening to Khon'Tor, Hakani was plotting. She doubted Adia would bring the offspring to the meeting at the beginning. That meant she would have it hidden somewhere safe and someone else would bring it at her signal. That someone could only be Nadiwani, and she would no doubt be waiting in the Healer's Chamber.

The only way Hakani could take control of the timing for what she had planned was to get the offspring herself. Once she did that, Adia and Nadiwani would know about the transgression of entering without permission, but relative to what was about to be revealed, Hakani gambled that her crime would pale in comparison. Regardless, she could see no other way.

She also realized Nadiwani would not hand the offspring over willingly. No matter; she was resolved to do whatever it took.

The People arrived ahead of the sounding of the assembly horn that always called everyone to a general meeting. There was much avid chatter and speculation. Even if the topic was most likely to be serious, there was still excitement that the Leader would be addressing the entire community.

Khon'Tor, Ogima Adoeete, and Is'Taqa were

seated together at the front of the Great Chamber as a sign of the solidarity between their tribes. Adia was sitting toward the front of the group. Not knowing what to do with Arina, she had brought her to the meeting, and they sat together. Looking around, Khon'Tor was not sure where Hakani was and thought it odd because she was usually at his side enjoying at every opportunity her elevated position as the Leader's mate.

Khon'Tor rose, and as he did, Ogima Adoeete and Is'Taqa rose with him. The Leader raised his hand to speak, at which point everyone immediately fell silent. All eyes were focused on him. It was as quiet in the Great Chamber as when it was completely vacant. The only sound was the water dripping down the sides of the walls.

"As you know, Ogima Adoeete and Is'Taqa of the Brothers, and I have returned from the High Council," started Khon'Tor, motioning toward the Chiefs standing to his right.

"We bring you greetings from the Leaders of the other tribes and communities. Unfortunately, the intent of the High Council meeting was not a happy one; this was not a time to discuss pairings or news of great harvests or to share gifts. It was instead a discussion and a planning session regarding a threat which faces our people as well as our friends, the Brothers," said Khon'Tor.

"Our People and the Brothers have lived in peace together for as long as we can remember. We have faithfully preserved the gifts of the Great Spirit, using them wisely, being grateful for the generosity of his provision. We have strived to keep the laws of our people, just as the Brothers have honored theirs. We have enjoyed generations of peace and relative prosperity as neighbors due to our shared beliefs and values. Unfortunately, not all those who walk among us share these same beliefs and values," he continued.

Khon'Tor stood rock still. He hardly ever walked around when he was speaking. He saw it as shifting and breaking the energy of his message.

"The Ancients foretold that conditions would change for us. They foresaw a time of trial, ushered in by intruders who would be unlike any of us, People and Brothers alike. That time is now on the horizon," he stated.

At that, a murmur rose up and spread through the crowd. Heads turned, and remarks were exchanged at the seriousness of this announcement. Khon'Tor gave them a moment to settle down.

The hall fell silent once more, and he began to speak again.

"Some of you have heard of the Waschini—the Whites as they call themselves. There are many names for them among us and the Brothers, and none of them are complimentary. From the reports we have, the Waschini live disconnected from the Great Spirit. They act in ways which demonstrate no respect for life; no sense of responsibility for the preservation of Etera, our world. They are cruel, brutal, self-serving. They murder females and offspring, and whatever else gets in their way.

"As heartless as they are, they are also unfortunately equally as intelligent. They have constructed tools and weapons far beyond our abilities. We do not know where they come from, but we know several of them have already arrived in the far coastal regions and they seem intent on extending their reach into our lands.

"The People, like the Brothers, choose peace whenever possible. We are not afraid of conflict, but we do not seek it out. Truly, we have never encountered another creature like the Waschini, with no boundaries to the evil of which they are capable. Because their souls—if they have them—are so alien to ours, we cannot allow ourselves to believe we understand them. We cannot allow ourselves to underestimate the potential devastation they bring. To do that might risk the final demise of the People."

After the earlier meeting, Adia had decided to leave Oh'Dar in the Healer's Quarters with Nadiwani. She had arranged for one of the females in her inner circle to fetch them if, after all, this seemed to be the right time. She knew she had to be very precise in the timing. She had to know when the other discussion was winding down, but not so far that the crowd started to dissipate. She tried to let go and trust it would work out as it should.

But the longer Khon'Tor talked, the worse Adia felt. From the picture Khon'Tor was painting, there were no redeeming qualities in the Waschini. She could feel the tension and alarm rising in the group. Her earlier faith in her timing collapsed, and right or wrong, she decided this would certainly *not* be the time to reveal the presence of Oh'Dar in their midst and confess her crime in bringing him here.

Adia caught the eye of the female, Kachina, who was to fetch Nadiwani and the offspring, and slowly shook her head, *"No."*

Kachina saw her and nodded that she understood.

No one in the crowd moved; their attention was fixed on Khon'Tor as he continued.

"I do not speak to alarm you. On nearly every level you wish to pick, the Waschini are no match for us. They seem to have no knowledge of the forest, and they have no sense when it comes to their use of the land or the medicines it provides. Their sense of direction is remarkably impaired, and physically they do not come even close to being a threat to us. But their intelligence and their soullessness *are* a threat, and for that, we must make preparations.

"We have learned through the generations that

the winning maneuver in a conflict is to avoid it in the first place. You know I am not a coward. You know that none of the High Council members are cowards. We are more than willing to take our place in battle if the time comes. But war comes with a great price; often an immeasurable price.

"The same Ancients who gave us the laws for our rightful and beneficial living saw this coming years ago. Wrak-Ayya, the Age of Shadows. We of the High Council have mapped out a plan, should it become inevitable. Wrak-Ayya will require us to change some of our ways, but we will implement those changes as slowly, yet as prudently as possible. We have adjusted to other changes; we will adjust to this one also—if it is what must be."

The murmur rose again within the crowd. Khon'Tor had known ahead of time that his words would have a great impact on his people. He hated to destroy their peace of mind, but he could not withhold such important information from them, either. It was his responsibility to look out for the People's welfare, and they deserved to know.

"I remind you of a truth you already possess—that change is the nature of all life. If and when the Waschini come, we will deal with them. We will seek guidance from the Great Spirit. And I assure you, if it comes to direct conflict with the Waschini, I will be the first to defend and protect our people at whatever personal cost."

Each time he paused, the clamor resumed.

Khon'Tor had a gift for speaking; he could move people's feelings and change their thinking. And when their thinking changed, their behavior followed accordingly.

Khon'Tor raised his hand again, immediately silencing the crowd, and continued.

"I do not intend for my words to alarm you. There may come a time for alarm, but this is not it. There have only been isolated sightings of them on our land. The Waschini are not at our door. And even if they were, again—"

Khon'Tor's speech was abruptly interrupted. All heads turned to follow a hurried movement rushing toward the front of the room. Suddenly standing beside him on the platform was Hakani, appearing as if out of nowhere and carrying something wrapped in a hide.

As everyone's heads snapped in her direction, Hakani stepped rudely in front of her mate, interrupting him and shouting over the clamor, "You are a great Leader Khon'Tor, my mate. And we are blessed by your wise leadership. But unbeknownst to you, a great wrong has been done to us. Not only has the Waschini already come to our land, it has been brought *here* among our very midst!"

Hakani hoisted the bundle in one hand, as high as she could, jerking the cover off to reveal Oh'Dar dangling helplessly overhead for all the People to see.

Ogima Adoeete, High Chief of the Brothers, had

been following every word of Khon'Tor's speech, nodding his agreement and showing his support. But confusion and alarm crossed his face when Hakani appeared on stage as if from nowhere, holding up the Waschini offspring.

Standing there, staring at Hakani, whose right hand held the offspring, raised over her head, Ogima Adoeete turned to Is'Taqa and asked, "What is Hakani, Third in Command, Mate to Khon'Tor, Leader of the largest Sasquatch tribe in the region, doing with a Waschini child?"

CHAPTER 6

Adia stood frozen as Hakani held Oh'Dar suspended dangerously overhead. Then without conscious volition, in one giant leap, she was on the stage facing Hakani, legs apart, standing directly between her and Khon'Tor.

Adia could hear the pandemonium break out—the volume, already loud, rose to deafening levels when she sprang onto the stage. She blocked everything out of her mind—her only thought was to protect the small, helpless offspring dangling from Hakani's upstretched hand.

Every part of her bristling with threat, Adia locked eyes with Hakani and carefully and menacingly leaned in toward her, her hands raised and stretched out to her side, blocking any route of escape Hakani might try.

A rumbling growl rose from her throat as she stared at Hakani. "Hand me the offspring, Hakani," she said. "Hand me the offspring carefully, or I swear I will gut you where you stand."

Everyone's eyes were wide; they had never seen Adia like this. Adia was the Healer, the counselor—not a warrior. No one had known she was capable of such fury. Her body was tensed, her eyes alert, ready to take any action necessary.

Whatever Hakani's plan had involved, it apparently did not include her own demise, and she slowly lowered the offspring and handed it carefully to Adia.

As soon as she had control of Oh'Dar, Adia cradled the offspring with her right arm and lunged at Hakani, grabbing her hair with her left hand and jerking her head back, exposing the soft flesh of Hakani's neck. The Healer pressed her sharp canines into the flesh for a moment and then drew back while Hakani clawed the air, trying to maintain her balance.

Adia hissed, "Threaten this offspring again, ever, or even enter the same room as him, and I will rip your throat to shreds, spit out the pieces, and gladly watch as you die in agony with your blood pouring out at my feet."

Adia released Hakani's hair and moved her hand to the female's throat, letting her sharp nails cut into the flesh, not caring if she left a mark.

Adia released Hakani as quickly as she had taken control of her, shoving her backward as she did. Hakani stumbled and fell to the ground. In that same movement, Adia turned swiftly to face Khon'Tor, her dark eyes still black with fury. She gave him the same low growl, her eyes locked on his, daring him to take a step closer to her and the offspring.

Khon'Tor was trying to figure out what was going on. Not only had his mate transgressed by rudely stepping in front of him, but she had contradicted him publicly. She had also completely derailed his intentions for the meeting.

And where the krell did that Waschini PetaQ come from?

In the next moment, his question was answered as he watched Adia cover the distance to Hakani in one lightning-fast bound. In a few seconds, she had recovered the screaming offspring and had Hakani in a death grip.

Khon'Tor had never seen such anger in Adia. He could tell she was one fraction of a thought away from opening Hakani's neck then and there, right in front of him, the Brothers' Chiefs, and the entire population of his people. He knew only a fool would underestimate the seriousness of her threat—or her intention to carry it out. The Healer of the People of the High Rocks had become a lethal weapon.

Equally quickly, she had released Hakani and turned to face him. Though he was immanently larger than her, and she did not pose the same physical challenge to him as a male of their community would, he knew by the look in her eyes that if he made one threatening move, she would expend her last breath protecting the offspring.

As Khon'Tor and Adia continued to square off, Is'Taqa and Ogima Adoeete stepped to the side. From the crowd, Arina ran to join them.

"Adia!" shouted Khon'Tor. Adia's eyes were fixed —as if nothing existed but the lock she had on Khon'Tor.

By now, Nadiwani had made it to the Great Chamber. She was holding a wrap to her forehead, a deep red stain of blood spreading through it. Gasping for breath, she entered the vast room to find—in place of a peaceful assembly—a room filled with highly agitated and nearly out-of-control fellow Sasquatch.

The last thing she remembered was Hakani entering the Healer's Quarters without warning and coming at her aggressively. When Nadiwani came to, her head was splitting, and she was bleeding profusely, a bloodied rock discarded a few feet from where she lay. But worse than any of that was the moment she realized Oh'Dar was missing. Though dizzy and disoriented from the blow to her head, she flew to the Great Chamber as quickly as she could.

"Adia! What are you doing? What is going on here? What is the meaning of all this?" Khon'Tor demanded.

Adia snarled at him again and stepped back, moving herself and the crying offspring into a more defensive position between Khon'Tor and Hakani.

At that moment, Nadiwani pushed her way to the front and her friend's side. Adia quickly glanced at her, saw how close she was, and passed Oh'Dar into the Helper's arms. By now, the offspring was crying even harder, and Nadiwani cradled and rocked him. Unencumbered by Oh'Dar, Adia now felt more confident.

The commotion in the crowd had shifted, the focus now intent on the drama unfolding in front of them between their three Leaders, Khon'Tor, Adia, and Hakani. Standing at her full height and not relaxing her offensive stance, Adia turned her attention back to Khon'Tor.

Out of the corner of her eye, she saw Khon'Tor's High Protector, Acaraho, moving slowly yet confidently toward the front of the room.

"Adia," began Khon'Tor again. "What is going on? What has happened? *What have you done?*"

The meeting was out of control. Khon'Tor was no longer in charge of what was happening, and Adia knew this was something he would not tolerate well.

"Khon'Tor," said Adia finally. "This is not how I wanted you to find out. I was going to come to you, come to this assembly, and explain. But then your *mate*," she continued, spinning her head to spit the word in Hakani's direction, "Your *mate* violated the sanctity of my quarters, abducted the offspring and executed her little drama just now, making everything worse." It was not like Adia to place blame on anyone else, but in this instance, she could not see it any other way.

"I will deal with that matter later, Adia. But for now, you owe me—you owe everyone—an explanation for why that spawn of the devil is in our midst.

"I brought the offspring to Kthama," she stated.

A gasp rolled through the crowd. The Healer of the People had just admitted to willfully breaking Second Law.

In the background, the Chief, Is'Taqa, and Nadiwani were monitoring the crowd, looking for any sign of collusion or a gathering of forces. Acaraho, the People's High Protector, was standing to the side, watching every move, his attention unwavering.

The room fell utterly silent as Adia went through her story—how she was on her way to deliver the Goldenseal to Ithua, Medicine Woman of the Brothers and Is'Taqa's sister. She explained about the river being up and her seventh sense telling her not to cross. She told of the setting she had found—the bloody, vicious massacre of the two Whites whom she assumed were the offspring's parents. She explained how she had discovered the offspring still alive and unharmed and had struggled over its fate, ultimately deciding she had to bring it back with her.

For Khon'Tor, matters were going from bad to worse. He had hoped there was an explanation of some extraordinary circumstance, but Adia had intentionally defied the laws of the People. When she was done, he had not heard the compelling reason he hoped to hear. This was not good for the community, and that meant it was also not good for his position as Leader.

"You should have left it to die, Adia. It was not our problem. You have broken one of the Second Laws. You have put the People at risk by bringing that monster here. I have no comprehension of what you were thinking," said Khon'Tor.

"The offspring is innocent, Khon'Tor," said Adia.

Her contradiction enraged him. The muscles in his jaw tightened, "The offspring is a monster. It should have died back there with its own kind.

"Were you not listening to anything I said? What the High Council has shared? The Waschini, if they are not our enemy now, soon enough will be. The path has been set. It is not our doing. It is theirs, by their soulless and evil nature. And you think to bring one *here*? To our very *home*?"

Khon'Tor made wide sweeping motions with his arms as he spoke. Hakani's behavior and now Adia's talking back at him were too much.

What is going on with the females in my community?

First Hakani and now Adia? But no, Hakani betrayed me openly. She physically attacked and hurt one of the People. Hers was the greater sin. And as revered as Adia is, if anything were to happen to her, I would be held responsible. I have already lost one Healer to tragedy— the last thing I need is for the High Council to get involved in this.

But at the moment he could only deal with the one overriding problem. "The offspring cannot stay. Either you return it to where you found it and let it meet its fate, or I will have someone else do it." He stood facing the Healer, his arms and legs staunchly tensed.

A standoff had been created. Adia's posture, which had relaxed a bit in telling the story, was now back in full offensive position. Adia was making it clear she had no intention of taking the offspring back to let it die, or of letting anyone else do so.

Some movement arose from the back of the room. Slowly, the crowd parted, letting four figures move forward. The females walked in unison to the front of the room—Donoma, Haiwee, Lomasi, and Mapiya. Everyone's eyes turned to watch them as they lined up between Nadiwani, who still held Oh'Dar, and Khon'Tor. The females' statement was clear. Khon'Tor then realized that some time must have passed between when Adia had brought the Outsider in and his return from the High Council meeting—giving her time to gain support for her actions.

Khon'Tor had to think quickly. Females were revered among the People. Their safety and protection were of the utmost importance. By effectively creating a barrier around the Healer's Helper and the offspring they were saying to him, *"We stand with her. Do you want to make this about* you *against* us? *Choose wisely."*

Several scenarios of how this could go ran through the Leader's head. None of them went in his favor.

They were only four females, but they were influential, and he knew the females of the People all shared a special bond. If he forced his point, he could well lose the favor of all the females of his community. If he lost favor with the females, the males would eventually turn against him—or at least blame him for the resulting miserable and uncomfortable state of their relationships. More than an icy silence or neglecting their roles and tasks, should they wish, the females had the right to refuse to mate. And it was one of the First Laws: Never Without Consent.

At the moment, Adia had violated only one of the Second Laws: No Contact With Outsiders. And being a female and the Healer, it would be a great deal to expect Adia to leave the offspring to die.

Khon'Tor knew that as Leader, he had the authority to take any tack he wanted. It was his decision, but the consequences would also be his. From his experience, in a direct confrontation based on a show of power, there were always two losers, not one. He had to buy some time by allowing both sides to back down without it looking like the females had won this round. Whatever else must happen between them had to take place outside of the public view.

"Clearly, this is a difficult situation," started Khon'Tor, feeling that this was an insipid opening statement. "There are strong beliefs on both sides. Much has happened here, and emotions are running high. I can see we will not come to a resolution now; therefore, I am calling for a moratorium.

"Adia, Nadiwani, and the Waschini will be allowed to return to the Healer's Quarters. I will place guards at the tunnel to protect them," he added, looking squarely at his mate, his eyes dark and cold.

His message to her was loud and clear. "*You are not innocent. I will deal with you later.*"

He looked over at Acaraho. As if on cue, the High Protector raised his hand and looked over to the left, and four very large Sasquatch males came forward. Though seldom needed, the People did have a group of males prepared to respond to a threat if necessary, and they fell directly under Acaraho's command.

Khon'Tor waited for them to reach the front of the room. When they were finally standing in front of him, the Leader addressed them, loud enough that everyone could hear.

"No one is allowed entrance to the Healer's Quarters except the Healer, the Helper, and these four females you see here."

As he said that, another female rose cautiously from the crowd and stepped forward. It was Oh'Dar's wet nurse, Pakuna.

Khon'Tor looked over at the younger female and then at Adia. Adia tilted her head in the female's direction as if to say, "*Her too.*"

Though not in a mood to grant Adia any favors, he growled to the guards, "And Pakuna also." He paused.

"Any other visitors must be brought in escorted by Adia or Nadiwani. They will be allowed to move freely at will, but the Waschini must remain in their quarters until we can address the situation further.

"*Anyone*," he said, "*Anyone* breaking these rules will suffer swift and serious consequences." And he glared in Hakani's direction.

Khon'Tor continued, still addressing the crowd. "This has been a trying day. It is not behind us yet; no doubt, more trying days will come before this is over. I urge you to seek a place of rest and allow your emotions to settle. Try to keep discussion among yourselves to a minimum so as not to fuel the fire regarding this turn of events. After I have considered all the arguments, I will convene another meeting and let you know of my decision.

"That is all," he finished, and raised his left hand overhead, palm forward, as his usual signal that the meeting had ended. He then stepped down, breaking eye contact with everyone; signaling that there would be no more discussion on the matter.

The crowd dissipated slowly. All those in the front, at the heart of the drama, stayed in place while the rest straggled out. When the Great Chamber was otherwise vacant, Adia took her leave with her accompaniment of females and guards in tow.

At the same time, the Chief and Is'Taqa approached Khon'Tor and said they were going to be on their way. This was clearly the People's business, and they both felt they were intruders and should never have witnessed such intimate events that were not of their village. Unnecessary to say it aloud, they had pledged their silence and discretion in the matter, as well as that of Arina. Though neither the Chief nor Is'Taqa was quite sure how Arina had gotten there, there would be time to hear the story on their way back to the village.

Khon'Tor nodded, and the three took their leave.

As the Brothers left, Hakani decided also to make her escape. She started to step away, and Khon'Tor reached out, grabbing her arm quickly and yanking her over to him, none too gently.

"Oh, no. Not you. *Not yet*," said Khon'Tor, one corner of his top lip curling up.

Khon'Tor released her arm, confident she would not try to leave. He turned away from her momentarily, running his hand up and back through the thick crop of silver hair that adorned his crown. He shook his head as if he could not wrap his mind around her actions.

"Hakani," he said, turning back to face her, "I do not know where even to begin. So why don't you start by explaining your actions here today."

Hakani offered up not one word. His directive meeting with silence instead of answers, Khon'Tor tried a different approach. "How long has the White Man's offspring been here?"

"About seven days."

"Have you and Adia already argued over this?"

"No."

"How did you find out about the offspring then?

Hakani stood without answering him, eyes lowered.

Khon'Tor was not stupid. He remembered her unusual friendliness with him the morning after his return, and he realized she must have been planning this whole debacle. It was not a spur of the moment act; she had intended it to be as disruptive as possible. But *who else had known and who had tipped her off about the offspring?*

He knew Hakani hated Adia. He still did not know why, but what he had not realized until now, was just how much she must also hate him, to create such a problem, such a spectacle, in front of the entire community. She had to know this would put him in an extremely difficult position—possibly a no-win one. Though that remained to be seen, he knew it would take a stroke of genius to find the middle ground and resolve this without permanently and perhaps irrevocably dividing the People.

Hakani stood quiet and subdued, not volunteering anything. Tired of this cat and mouse game, Khon'Tor turned away and dismissed her with a wave of his hand, but not without turning back to deliver a fierce look, letting her know it was not over yet.

His glare spoke volumes. *The next time they spoke, he would expect real answers, and would not allow his questions to be answered with a deceptive wall of silence.*

Everyone had left, and Khon'Tor was alone in the Great Chamber. He had no desire to return to his quarters; the ones he shared with his traitorous mate. Adrenaline subsiding, the physical and mental strain suddenly overtook him. He was suddenly tired; so very tired.

Not knowing where to go, and fatigued beyond measure, Khon'Tor, Leader of the People of the High Rocks, exited the great cave of his people. He stood looking up at the peaceful, dark sky for a few moments, then found a secluded grassy spot, stretched out his full eight feet and fell asleep under the canopy of stars.

◌

In the Healer's Quarters, Nadiwani and Adia checked over Oh'Dar before turning in. Nadiwani made him a calming poultice and gave him a small dose of

Ginseng Root tincture to help him relax and fall asleep.She spent a while holding and rocking him, and eventually, he calmed down. She hated that he had been traumatized. It was bad enough that a stranger had stolen him from her arms, then apparently hoisted him roughly and precariously above the others with no comforting support, but the resulting chaos and din had even further frightened him. Adia had been in such a towering rage that she had not realized how terrified Oh'Dar was. *It's just as well because had she, Adia might full well have gone ahead and killed Hakani right there in front of everyone.*

As she looked at the sleeping offspring, Nadiwani realized how much, the Waschini and the Brothers resembled each other; they were both frail and slight with virtually no hair, except for a ridiculous collection on the top of their heads. No wonder they both fashioned wrappings to cover themselves; she had often thought they must always be cold.

In truth, the Brothers and the People also had similarities. Their underlying skin tones were close, and though the People were slightly darker, their facial features were not dissimilar. The most marked difference was in size and strength, and the People had large, sharp canines—which were only really visible when they were snarling or growling.

The People's fine down hair covering was also not that evident on first notice, though the males' chest hair was fuller, as well as that around their hip areas, making the need for loincloths or other wrappings generally unnecessary. With very few having the heavier body hair of the males, most of the females traditionally wore wrappings, especially those who had sparser body hair, or fairer coloring.

In spite of Oh'Dar's unnaturally pale skin and his spindly, hairless body, he no longer looked as alien to Nadiwani as he had at first. She was starting to think he was so ugly he was almost cute. Those sky-blue eyes, his sweet disposition, and endearing smile had helped her see past *what* he was to *who* he was. As she cuddled him and held him close, she realized she did indeed care for this pathetic, awkward seed of the White monsters.

To her surprise, Adia found the guards posted outside the tunnel to her quarters to be a comfort. In no way did she feel she or Nadiwani were prisoners. She accepted at face value that Khon'Tor had placed the guards there for protection and no other reason. Knowing Hakani could not violate her quarters again helped her relax, and a bit of their comforting and sanctified atmosphere was restored.

Adia knew it would not be long before Khon'Tor called for her. At least, that was what she surmised; he had just bought himself time and moved the altercation out of the public eye to where he could figure out what to do without the entire community witnessing the process. She also knew information might surface about which he would not want all the People to know.

Looking back, she realized how very deeply it must have enraged Khon'Tor when Hakani took over the meeting. He hated to lose control, and she could only imagine the state he was in by the time it was over. She almost felt sorry for him.

Try as she might, Adia could not figure out why Hakani would set her up this way. She knew Khon'-Tor's mate did not care for her, though she had never understood why; but to create such a scene, to instill such turmoil among their People, and to create such great problems for Khon'Tor? *Hakani must have had a very good reason for it—or a very bad one. I doubt she cares one way or the other about Oh'Dar. It was just a way to cause trouble—but to what end?*

Hakani woke in their bed and realized Khon'Tor had not returned to their quarters. Where he had slept, she had no idea. As the night deepened, she realized he was not coming and felt a huge sense of relief. She knew she still had to face his anger but was grateful for the chance to get a little sleep first. She had not slept well the night before, busy honing her plot to steal the Waschini offspring.

She wondered how Khon'Tor was going to decide the punishment for her and the Healer. Knowing him as she did, she suspected he would call a meeting with all of them and get everything out at once. Hakani hoped she would be smart enough to see his questions coming but knew she had crossed a line that could not be uncrossed.

Her relationship with Khon'Tor had never been a good one, but at least up until now, there had not been out and out war between them. How quickly things had gone downhill. She could still remember standing next to him when he chose her as his mate, excitedly looking forward to an enjoyable relationship with this strong, compelling Alpha male.

CHAPTER 7

The next morning, the community was abuzz with talk about the previous day's events. Mostly there was shock at the idea that a Healer could break one of the People's laws, but opinions were divided. Some defended Adia, but others were against her, citing that there was no excuse for someone in her position of authority to violate any of the People's laws. Nobody remembered a time when anyone in any of the three direct positions of authority—Leader, Healer, or Leader's Mate —had intentionally broken any of the laws. In particular, it was shocking that it could be Adia. She was among the most highly respected Healers of any of the People's communities, known for her strong connection to the Great Mother—which reinforced the opinions of those who firmly believed she must have had an excellent reason for her actions.

By late morning, Khon'Tor had called for them. Acaraho, the High Protector, came down to escort Adia and Nadiwani to the rooms that were located off one of the Great Chamber tunnels and used for smaller meetings.

He had brought Donoma with him to stay and care for Oh'Dar. Adia trusted Donoma but was uneasy about leaving Oh'Dar behind. Still, she knew the offspring's presence would be inflammatory. Perhaps it was just as well that this should take place without him being there. Adia and Donoma exchanged a few private words before Adia joined Nadiwani to follow quietly behind Acaraho. She was glad to see the two original guards still at their stations outside her quarters. She was confident that no one would be able to get through them; they stood a good seven feet tall and were broad-shouldered, stalwart.

Acaraho was even bigger than they. As the People's High Protector, he held a position of great authority and responsibility. A leftover from earlier times of conflict, the position had survived within their community structure. Though there was presently no direct threat requiring an organized army, Acaraho commanded the males under him in performing specialized duties other than those of the guards and watchers, as needed.

Considering Acaraho's reputation and high rank,

Adia realized Khon'Tor had assigned his best guard to protect them as they walked to the meeting. She doubted it was solely for their welfare; it was more likely that he did not want one more thing disrupting his control of the situation.

The last thing Khon'Tor needs is for word of problems between his Second and Third Rank to get back to the High Council. He cannot risk misjudging just how far Hakani might go to make further trouble. Khon'Tor is not a trusting man; I do believe Acaraho might be the only one he does trust.

Adia's eyes remained on the High Protector as he escorted them to the meeting room. He was easily as tall as Khon'Tor, and in equally good physical condition. Even by the People's standards, he was, in a word, *huge,* and she doubted anyone could get to her or Nadiwani through him. His eyes were always in motion, sizing up his surroundings.

A massive chest, deeply defined muscles rippling underneath his light covering of dark hair, warm yet strong, with deeply set dark eyes—all these worked together to make him uncommonly attractive. Whenever Adia was around him, Acaraho always conducted himself stoically, never making eye contact unless delivering a specific message.

Luckily, by the time Adia and Nadiwani reached the room, the others were already assembled, and the meeting was ready to start as soon as Khon'Tor arrived. Adia did not trust herself alone with Hakani very long—something Khon'Tor had no doubt been wise enough to realize when he engineered each of the arrivals.

I wonder what Acaraho's reaction would be should I lose control and attack Hakani here and now?

The room was large, like everything at Kthama, but not cavernous. Smooth boulders of various sizes were placed in a semi-circle for seating, as meetings could often stretch out longer than was advantageous to stand around or sit on the ground. As with most of the other rooms, there was only one entrance. A guard had been placed outside, and Acaraho was positioned inside the meeting room.

Adia was pleased Khon'Tor had chosen Acaraho to be present, though it meant he would overhear everything discussed. Adia dismissed that from her mind, relying on Khon'Tor's judgment and what she knew: Acaraho was a male of discretion. Despite whatever else she was feeling at the moment, she did respect and admire Khon'Tor in many ways. Accepting the job Acaraho was there to do, she put his somewhat distracting presence out of her mind.

Both Nadiwani and Adia had spent time that morning appealing to the Mother for help and guidance. They had also each taken a tincture of the same Ginseng Root Nadiwani had given to Oh'Dar, to help them stay calm.

It was not long after they were all seated that Khon'Tor entered. The silver shock of hair on the top of his head made his identity unmistakable.

Khon'Tor had slept outside under the stars the night before, but he'd had enough time to gain control of his reactions. Despite the tumultuous clamoring of the emotions created from yesterday's events, he had managed to harness them all and sublimate them into one stone-cold, hard, physical presence that bristled with authority and power.

The Leader walked around behind them in carefully measured and controlled steps, his hands clasped behind his back. His circling behind them was a show of domination. Every move he made emphasized his authority as Leader and sent them each a crystal-clear message. *That their transgressions were severe, that he and he alone was in charge here, that his judgment of them would be final, and would not and could not be challenged.*

Khon'Tor finally took his place, standing in front of the semi-circle where they were seated. There was a boulder placed there for him, should he wish to sit. Before he said a word, he took a moment to make eye contact with each of them, starting at the far left where Nadiwani was seated, moving to Adia, and then to his mate, Hakani, on the right.

Though the actions of each angered him, he was *furious* with his mate.

Having achieved his objective in establishing his position of power, Khon'Tor now sat down facing them. Legs spread, fists pressing down on the tops of his knees, sitting rigid and upright, he was the very picture of controlled power.

His eyes were cold, "Each of you will be granted an equal amount of time to make your case in defense of your actions. After I have heard you out, I will make my decision regarding the punishment for those actions."

Nadiwani glanced fleetingly at Adia as Khon'Tor made use of the word 'punishment'. No one spoke. Seconds passed. Khon'Tor let the silence grow. In this setting, unlike yesterday's debacle in the Great Chamber, he was in complete control.

He had hardened his heart and felt no compunction at all for their discomfort. Quite the converse— he was enjoying it.

Khon'Tor turned to Nadiwani first, locking his gaze on her. Nadiwani was the Healer's Helper; she was not used to being in the line of fire, was not established as a Leader in the community. She had not needed to develop a steely mental core or the level of defensive offense the others had, and she had no experience with issues of this magnitude. She immediately looked down, unconsciously signaling her surrender.

"Nadiwani. I believe your role in this to be one of default. If I am wrong and you were instrumental in bringing this *Waschini* offspring into our community, I expect you to speak now and accept responsibility for your actions."

Adia spoke up, trying to protect Nadiwani, "Nadiwani is not at fault here. She—"

Without moving his head or even glancing in Adia's direction, Khon'Tor extended his arm, with his palm facing toward her, and cut the Healer off midsentence. "I did not ask *you*, woman. I am asking the girl, Nadiwani."

His use of these terms was intentional. Though females were revered by the People, this was a direct dismissal of their official positions within the community. He was sending every message he could that his was the only power here.

Nadiwani swallowed hard. "Though I was not directly involved in bringing the offspring here," she said, replacing his degrading choice of the word 'Waschini' with the kinder term, "I have willfully participated in his care and protection. I stand with Adia; do with me what you will."

Nadiwani's response surprised Khon'Tor. He had felt her surrender earlier under his gaze but now respected her for standing up to him. However, this was not the time to let her or any of the others know that.

"Is that all you have to say?" asked Khon'Tor coldly.

"My statement stands as I have given it," replied Nadiwani.

Not willing to discharge any of the tension in the room by letting Nadiwani off the hook in any regard, Khon'Tor turned to Hakani, bypassing Adia and breaking the order they all assumed he would follow. He wanted to keep them on edge.

Though she was officially Third Rank by her station as the Leader's mate, Hakani was no match for Khon'Tor in a direct one-on-one confrontation. She was wily and clever, and skillfully deceitful—all attributes she employed in trying to stay one step ahead of him. But in a direct contest of wills or personal force of character, Khon'Tor was the winner, hands down. Hakani had hoped Khon'Tor's anger would be somewhat dissipated by the time he got to her, but in truth, no amount of time could have eased his ire.

Khon'Tor turned to address her.

"How and when did you learn of the offspring?" he asked, repeating the question she had partially sidestepped the afternoon before. Hakani shifted in her seat, stalling. Khon'Tor stared at her. *Now is your chance; I suggest you take it and explain yourself.*

"I learned of the offspring on the night of Adia's return. I entered the Healer's Quarters uninvited while they were sleeping and discovered the offspring."

At that admission, Adia involuntarily inhaled sharply. Hakani had breached the sanctity of the Healer's Quarters. Not only that, but she had entered at a time when both Adia and Nadiwani were defenseless, lost in sleep. It was a cowardly act because no one of honor would violate another when that other was helpless. Sleep was a time when the soul rejoined the Great Spirit. All sleeping quarters were considered sacred spaces.

Having answered Khon'Tor's question, Hakani paused.

There were a hundred questions he wanted to ask her. *Why did you pick such a moment to reveal the offspring's presence? Why did you not come to me directly when there were many opportunities for you to tell me in private? What was your intention in acting so? Who was the real target of your actions? Me? Adia? Everyone?* And lastly, *Why do you hate Adia so?*

But he asked none of them. He did not expect that Hakani would answer, and no matter what she said, he had already made up his mind about her guilt, even if he did not understand her motivations.

"You violated the Healer's Quarters. You attacked the Healer's Helper, drawing blood. You kidnapped an offspring and brought chaos and turmoil to an already inflammatory situation. What do you offer in defense of your actions?" he asked Hakani.

"I offer no defense," said Hakani.

Oddly enough, at that moment, Khon'Tor believed she was speaking the truth. Whether it was evidence of some remorse on her part or simply a statement of fact that there was indeed no valid defense possible, he was not sure.

Khon'Tor sat for a little while, his elbows now resting on his knees, his hands intertwined in front of him. He closed his eyes and lowered his head for a few seconds, creating a moment of privacy in which to collect his thoughts.

It was Adia's turn.

Wanting to reassert her position of power, Adia did not wait for Khon'Tor's permission to speak. While she was waiting, she had been praying to the Mother for wisdom and eloquence and that the power of her words would come from the power of the truth—whatever that might be—and not from her belief in the ultimate righteousness of her actions.

Khon'Tor nullified her attempt to regain some ground by not acknowledging she had already taken it upon herself to speak up. He turned his head in her direction as she started to speak, implying that he had been waiting impatiently for her to begin. When it came to executing moves and counter-moves, Khon'Tor was the master.

"I accept full responsibility for my actions," began Adia. This was not an attempt to placate Khon'Tor's anger. It was a statement of fact, and indeed, it stood on its merits.

Yesterday, in the meeting hall in front of every-one, Adia had already explained how she set out to deliver the Goldenseal roots to Ithua, Medicine Woman of the Brothers. She had explained how she came across the horrific scene and discovered the offspring, and that she had then brought him back with her. She now continued the story.

"When I first found the slaughtered bodies of the

offspring's parents, I was horrified and dumbstruck at the cruelty and viciousness of their dispatch. Even the state in which they were left dead and lifeless spoke to the soullessness of whoever murdered them. They were splayed out where they were struck down, allowing them no dignity in their final moments, left with no regard to their exposure to the elements or to the predators of the forest who feed on such carrion. The brutality and heartlessness of the scene sickened me to my core. Both of them, male and female, had obviously been made to suffer before they died. The hair coverings on both their heads had been sliced away and removed. Clearly, there had been a struggle. Signs indicated the female had been taken Without Her Consent—whether before or after her death, I do not know."

Adia continued, "Whoever did this tried to make it look as if the Brothers committed these unspeakable acts, but I know that was not the case. The tracks left by the riders leading to and from the scene were those of the White Men. Two perfectly healthy horses were left tethered to a strange structure. Not only are the Brothers incapable of such wanton cruelty, but none of their tribes would have left the horses, as valuable as they are."

Everyone in the room except Khon'Tor, who was withholding any and all reaction to her story, was unconsciously nodding agreement at her assessment that none of the Brothers could have committed this.

"There are no words to express my level of

disgust and despair—how horrified I was to come across this scene. I knew it was the work of the Waschini. I said a prayer for the souls, but there was nothing else I could do for them. As I was preparing to leave, I heard a noise. My heart sank as I realized something else was still alive at the scene. Fearing the worst of what I would find, I looked inside the compartment to which the horses had been tethered. It was there I found the offspring." Adia made a point of using the word, just as Nadiwani had.

"I am not proud of my first reaction. This was a Waschini offspring, spawn of the same soulless race that had committed these abhorrent acts. As a Healer, I had no right to feel as I did; I considered killing it on the spot. Had I done so, at that moment, I would have felt fully justified. Here was a soulless creature just waiting to grow up and inflict more pain and suffering in our world. Why would I not take this moment to dispatch it quickly, before it could bring the evil acts to bear which no doubt rested in its soul —if it had one? It would be kinder to kill it quickly rather than leaving it to die of exposure, or worse. Though, based on the sins of its kind, I even considered whether it deserved to be spared pain or suffering."

Up until now, Adia had been sitting level with Khon'Tor. But now she stood up, walking behind the others, placing them between her and Khon'Tor, and creating a show of unity with the females of the People.

"I love the People. I would never do anything to bring harm or dishonor to our community. I would never bring dishonor to you, Khon'Tor. Trust me when I tell you now, to have killed the offspring would have done all that," she said.

"I am not defending the Waschini by any means. I would never, ever do that. Their record stands for itself. Those who commit these acts deserve the severest of punishments, even including death. None of us would argue otherwise. But at that moment, there was no Waschini in front of me; there was only an offspring, helpless, unable to defend or care for itself. Its life was in my hands; whether I killed it myself or left it to die, the decision was the same." She paused for just a moment.

"Khon'Tor, you spoke of my violation of the Second Law: No Contact With Outsiders. It is on that crime that you are no doubt deciding my fate. But the offspring has committed no crime unless you deem its very existence a crime. It has committed no bad acts. It does not have hatred or evil in its heart. I am not innocent; not one of us in this room is innocent. Not even you, Khon'Tor. But I speak this truth from the hearts of all females everywhere; no offspring enters the world carrying sin. We are all guilty and deserving of judgment, but an offspring is not. An offspring, *all offspring* are born innocent. We have always recognized their innocence until they reach the age of accountability."

With that, Adia stopped speaking and looked into

Khon'Tor's eyes. She was appealing to his higher nature with all her soul, praying her words had reached him. Praying he would respond to her and see her as a female first, and not as someone who had betrayed the laws of the People; not as someone who had betrayed him.

There was not a sound in the room.

Though Khon'Tor would never admit it, Adia's words had their effect. He did realize that what she said was true—the offspring was still innocent. And because it was innocent, he could not condemn it to death. Nor could he condemn her for saving it. To expect her to do otherwise would have been against everything she as a Healer, or as a female, represented. It would contradict the best to which any of them could aspire.

But he still had the problem of the offspring in their midst, and the danger it represented. He had to address those issues before he could decide their fate.

Still seated, Khon'Tor took over.

"I do not deny the horror of what you experienced. I do not deny the difficulty of your decision to let it live. Nor am I denying *or* admitting the validity of your position. But there are other factors to consider. The presence of this offspring creates a danger to all the People. It is an encumbrance. It is weak and frail and will never be able to function as a contributing member of our community. It will never be allowed to leave, so it will spend the rest of its life here. What will become of it when it reaches pairing age? When it is filled with a male's natural desires? None of the females will have it—so pitiful and repulsive. It will never be a provider or a protector. It will live and die alone, separated from its own kind. That is the life to which you have sentenced it, Adia. That is the life to which you have condemned it. Death would have been a kindness."

Tears were welling in Adia's eyes. The room was quiet; the atmosphere of fear had been replaced with an atmosphere of growing reverence. Healers believed reverence was carried on the wings of truth. Because when words of truth were spoken, they brought in the presence of the Great Spirit.

"I will take responsibility for the offspring, Khon'-Tor. The burden will be mine." She said it quietly, in keeping with the almost sacred feeling of the moment.

"Yes," replied Khon'Tor, "the responsibility *will* be yours, Adia. And since it was your decision alone to bring it here, you alone will shoulder the burden of raising it. It will be your responsibility to ensure it becomes a functioning member of this community. Its crimes will be your crimes. Its punishments will be your punishments. Whatever comes of this will be on your head. You may have the assistance of your Helper, Pakuna, and two of the four females who stood with you yesterday. But," he paused for effect and added in an even more steely voice, "if at any time I see the offspring as a threat—to the community as a whole or to any member of this community —*I will end its life myself.*"

When he first started speaking, Adia had some hope of a bearable outcome. But his final degree that she alone would be responsible for raising the offspring created a nearly impossible situation. How could she fulfill her role as Healer and raise an offspring—especially one about whom they knew so little? Nadi-wani and the others had their own responsibilities. In the People's communities, the rearing of offspring was shared by all. He had virtually ensured that her burden in this would be debilitating.

Quieted now, Adia knew she had not thought all of this through when she acted; she had acted out of the voice of her heart and not her head. Her heart, that for which the People most valued her other than her knowledge and skills as their Healer, had now become a liability and perhaps would bring times of terrible struggle to herself and all her people. And also to Oh'Dar.

But what of the clear vision she had received, that the offspring was tied to something important for the future of her people, that her finding him had not been an accident but the guidance of the Great Spirit?

"Khon'Tor," she started, "To place all of this on me is not fair to the offspring. Even with the others' help, the offspring will go without a great deal that he needs to fulfill your other decrees. He will have no father. The offspring of the People are always raised by all of the community."

"First of all," said Khon'Tor, "*It* is not an offspring of the People, and it has no rights to the contributions of any others. Secondly, if it suffers, it will not be my fault. It will be *yours*. The Waschini is your responsibility now."

With that, the discussion was closed. Khon'Tor got up to leave. He had made his decision, and Adia had to live with it. And his statement was not lost on her that if at any time he decided Oh'Dar was a threat, he would kill the offspring himself, without warning or second thought.

As Khon'Tor reached the door, he turned and addressed the group.

"There will be a general assembly tonight, after the evening meal, at which I will announce to the rest of the community my rulings in this regard. I suggest you all be there."

And with that, he left without a backward glance. Nobody spoke as they got up to go. Nadiwani took Adia's arm, and they walked out together. Acaraho followed behind the two, intentionally placing himself between them and Hakani.

Forgotten at the back of the room, Acaraho had witnessed everything through the eyes of someone with no personal stake in the proceedings. Three things struck him. First was the undeniable power of Khon'Tor, second only to his ability to make everyone uncomfortably aware of it. Thirdly, the visceral presence of the male was intimidating. Not just his distinct physical characteristics, but his body language, which he used expertly to convey his iron will.

This admission of Khon'Tor's commanding presence was coming from his physical equal. But though Acaraho shared Khon'Tor's physical strength, he was not consumed with the need to exert his will over others, as was Khon'Tor.

Acaraho had been moved by Adia's speech. Whatever he had thought before of the Healer's actions in bringing the offspring here, he now saw it through different eyes. He felt sorry for her, though he knew she would not want his pity. More importantly, he respected and agreed with her decision. He realized his opinion was of no importance in the matter, but he knew that if the others—the other males—could have heard her speak, they might feel differently about what she had done, as he now did.

On the way, escorting them back to their quarters, he wondered what would become of Hakani as nothing had been said about her punishment.

Hakani was wondering that herself. She had known going into it that there would be consequences for her actions. She had hoped Khon'Tor's anger with her would be overshadowed by his resultant anger with Adia. The fact that Khon'Tor did not question Hakani more thoroughly told her that whatever she said would not have changed anything. He had already made up his mind about the nature of her motivations. She did not think he knew what they were—only that he did not want to waste time hearing her excuses. He knew she had acted with malicious intent.

And though Khon'Tor had not declared any ruling on her actions, she knew that did not mean she had escaped his judgment—or his wrath. She was not naive enough to think she had avoided it, or that it would be merciful.

It would not be long before Hakani would find out just how right she was.

CHAPTER 8

A dia and Nadiwani followed the twists and turns of the corridors that brought them to their quarters, arriving safely under Acaraho's protection. Adia now could not help wondering what his thoughts were, having witnessed all this as an outsider. She sensed no judgment from him as he walked behind them. Oddly enough, she felt something more akin to compassion.

When they reached their quarters, Adia and Nadiwani went directly to Donoma, into whose care Oh'Dar had been entrusted. They found both resting quietly, Oh'Dar sound asleep in his area, the brown bear-like toy Adia had saved tucked up against him. If Donoma thought anything peculiar about the toy, she kept her opinion to herself.

Both Adia and Nadiwani were exhausted, both lost in thought and reeling from the repercussions of Khon'Tor's decision. Neither one of them wanted to think about it anymore. They both desperately needed rest. There would be time enough later to grapple with the weight of what he had saddled on Adia.

And there was still the assembly that evening to get through.

As Adia lay down gratefully on her sleeping mat, she wondered if the other females thought the same thing as Nadiwani had on first seeing the Waschini toy—that it carried a resemblance to the Nu'numic Sarnonn, the giants that some suspected might still exist in other regions. As far as the People were aware, the White Wasters knew nothing of the Nu'numic's existence—it was most likely coincidental, the toy fashioned after the common forest bears.

Hulking giants, far larger than her people, the Sarnonn were said to be covered in a much heavier coat and had a thicker build and more solid features. Their spoken language was supposedly guttural and deep in register. Their use of Handspeak was believed to be functional but rudimentary, as they would not have the finer dexterity of either the Brothers or the People. The People had not seen a Sarnonn in generations.

Adia's People, though they and the Brothers still considered them to be Sasquatch, were not as large and had more delicate features. In many ways, they looked like a mix between the Brothers and the ancient descriptions of the Nu'numic Sasquatch. The People still easily towered over the Brothers and they still possessed far superior strength and speed, but taking away those attributes and eliminating how disconcerting the sheer size of the males was, they could be considered attractive by the Brothers' standards.

There were ancient stories about why there were different strands of Sasquatch. The People and the Sarnonn did not share identical bloodlines, but the true story of the two lines was buried in the dark period of their history, the knowledge of which was passed down only to a select few.

Back in the Leader's Quarters, Khon'Tor was waiting for his mate. He was not only waiting for her; he was ready for her. He was standing to the side of the entrance, hidden from view, confident she would be along shortly—where else was there for her to go?

As Hakani entered, Khon'Tor abruptly stepped out behind her. She swirled to face him, his height rising nearly two feet over hers. Whatever he decided to do to her, or virtually anyone else for that matter, there would be no stopping him.

Hakani froze while Khon'Tor walked around, and standing behind her placed one hand firmly on each of her shoulders, moving as close to her as he could without actually touching. He was bristling with anger, and he felt his mate stiffen in fear, offering not the slightest movement or resistance.

"Khon'Tor—" she started.

"*Shut up, Hakani.* The time for your words is over! I think you already know why I did not ask you any questions in there. But in case you have any doubt, let me make it perfectly clear. I now see you for what you are—a liar and a troublemaker, not worthy of the trust I have placed in you. And certainly not worthy of the position of authority you hold as my mate.

"Whatever the reasons for what you did, they are utterly without merit. Nothing can justify the harm you did to our people. *My people.* Whatever goodwill there was in me toward you is gone. Your conduct displayed utter disregard for the needs or the good of this community. By that measure, you have no right to a position of any authority, over *anyone.* Your position as my partner, my counsel, is now in name only. As the consequences for your actions, including your attack on Nadiwani, I revoke your authority as third in command."

He paused to make sure she was listening to him. She was.

"I will allow you to continue living here with me, but I no longer require your fulfillment of your duties as my mate toward my care and well-being. Nor do I desire them. You live to fulfill one purpose and one purpose only for me now," and with that, Khon'Tor closed the little distance remaining between them and pressed his body firmly up against her back.

"Your one and only function from this moment forward is to provide me with offspring. Up until now, I have respected your refusal of me. While I do not have the right to force myself on you Without Your Consent, I strongly suggest you start giving it."

It was as close to a threat as he could get without crossing the line.

Khon'Tor was not done with her. He increased the pressure against her. Then, to make his next point even clearer, he removed one hand from her shoulders and encircled her waist with his arm, pressing himself up against her even harder.

He assumed he was on the verge of hurting her but did not care.

"You may, of course, continue to withhold your consent, which is your right. But if you do, I will exercise my rights and approach the High Council for Bak'tah-Awhidi. Once you are set aside as First Choice, I will take another mate—one who will be willing to provide me with the offspring you would deny me. Do not think my resolve on this matter will soften. I have let your refusal of me go on too long. You have exhausted your last chance of my mercy." And with that, Khon'Tor released her abruptly and left, leaving her to think about his warning.

Hakani almost collapsed after he let her go. She could not believe what she was hearing. He was withdrawing himself from her completely—from any relationship with her other than using her as a vessel for his seed. It had not occurred to her that she might lose it all—his confidence in her, her role as his mate, her position as third in command. Of it all, losing her rank was the worst. Having lost her status, she had nothing left that mattered to her.

Things had gone from bad to worse. In her hatred of Adia and her wish to discredit the Healer in Khon'Tor's eyes and the eyes of the People, she had underestimated the consequences of her actions. Her emotions had clouded her judgment.

She had pushed him too far.

As it stood now, she had only one role left to provide for him. And it was one that out of spite she had vowed early on never to fulfill—that of bearing his offspring.

Khon'Tor's threat of Bak'tah-Awhidi was very real and was within his rights to request. The People were not polygamous, but the Leader had an obligation to produce a blood heir. There were provisions to allow the complete setting aside of a pairing with cause, or if the problem was one of infertility, of allowing the Leader to take a second mate. The bloodlines of the People's leadership had never been broken.

If the Leader did not produce an heir, one could be chosen from a sibling's offspring, but Khon'Tor had no siblings. The next Leader of the People *had* to come through Khon'Tor. He could get rid of Hakani if she refused to allow him to mate her.

"First Choice," she said to Khon'Tor, though he had left the room. "First Choice," she said again. "I was never your First Choice, Khon'Tor!" and she spat at the open door through which he had just left. "And you know it. You just do not know that I know it —and have almost from the start."

Had he still been in the room to hear it, Khon'Tor would have gotten the answer to the question that had confounded him for so long—why did Hakani hate Adia so much?

Somewhere along the way, Khon'Tor had been careless. Somewhere along the way, there had been too many unguarded moments where he had let his feelings toward Adia show. It could have been a moment where he was caught up in watching her, forgetting others were in the room. Regardless, Hakani had learned it was Adia who had been in his heart, and not her. The fact that he seemed to carry animosity toward Adia meant nothing. She knew that love spurned often turned to hatred. In her mind, the two emotions were only a hair's breadth apart from each other.

When she figured this out, Hakani began to hate him just as he seemed to hate Adia. It was not that his affection was so important to her—it was that she knew she was not his First Choice. And somewhere from that place within herself, she imagined Adia to be a threat, though she had never seen the Healer express any interest toward Khon'Tor in return.

Besides which, Adia was the Healer and forbidden to mate.

She was incensed by the realization that she did not have the influence over Khon'Tor that she believed to be her right as a female. It was her hatred of Adia, wanting to see the Healer humiliated and brought down in front of Khon'Tor that had driven her to where she was now.

But Hakani had an incredible knack for turning defeat into victory. Thinking for a moment, she said to herself, "Well, Adia, I will have the last laugh after all. You may still be Second Rank, and I may lose my official rank entirely because of you—but there is one position I can hold that is even more powerful than yours. I did not see this before." And with that, Hakani spoke out loud the words, Asdza Ayashe Aama—Mother Of His Offspring.

The females who usually gathered to prepare the evening meal were huddled together, astir with conversation. What had Khon'Tor decided about the Waschini offspring, the Healer, and his mate's inexplicable behavior? Word had spread that he would be addressing everyone tonight after the meal was over, which raised conjecture to an even higher level.

As caretakers of the young, the females had quickly come to see the Waschini offspring as Adia saw him: the innocent victim of an unfortunate circumstance. They looked at his needs from their natural inclination to respond to the weak and help-less. Waschini or not, they had the same urge to care for him as they would feel the need to help a wounded fawn or wolf cub.

Donoma, Haiwee, Lomasi, and Mapiya, the four females whom Adia had taken into her inner circle, listened to the conversations intently—not trying to sway them, only trying to get a feel for their support of the Healer. The four agreed that the other females were overwhelmingly in favor of Adia, not only because of her role as Healer but perhaps also because they knew she was deprived by law of having her own offspring. Aside from the fact that the offspring was nearly unbearably ugly, maybe this was the Mother's way of letting Adia fulfill a female's natural yearnings for an offspring to care for.

If the opinion was going in Adia's favor, it was going against Hakani. No matter how they looked at it, the females could see no reason for Hakani to have created such a spectacle. They could find no justifi-cation for her not going to Khon'Tor in private to tell him what she had discovered. They all saw her disruptive actions as disrespectful to Khon'Tor—not only as Leader but also as her mate.

Regardless of Adia's breaking of the law against contact with Outsiders, they saw her motivation as coming from love. On the other hand, Hakani's moti-vation was entirely self-serving.

No matter how they spun it, the consensus was

that the drama Hakani had caused was somehow its own reward. But why she would want to create such trouble for the Healer and for her mate, they could not fathom.

○

That evening, unaware that Hakani had found a way to twist her defeat into victory, and thinking he had her back under his control, Khon'Tor went to the community meal feeling he had very effectively turned the situation around.

Now he had only to announce his decisions to the assembly, while also making it clear the subject was not open to any more discussion. After yesterday's debacle, it was vital that he reassert his power and leave no doubt about who was truly in control.

Khon'Tor scanned the room. Adia, Nadiwani, and Hakani were all noticeably absent from the shared evening meal. It did not surprise or alarm him. He imagined they were avoiding the inevitable questions about how they were doing, what they thought was going to happen, and more. However, just as the meal was ending, he saw Adia and Nadiwani enter the hall together, escorted by High Protector Acaraho. *At least they had the good sense not to bring the Waschini offspring.*

Still conspicuously missing was Hakani. *No matter. She will be here. She is not one to miss important events, especially when they concern something as crucial as her position of authority.*

Khon'Tor waited until everyone was done eating, and the leavings had been cleared away. He demanded everyone's full attention and nothing less.

As he was about to get up and start the session, Hakani entered from the tunnel that led to their quarters. He imagined this meant that after their 'talk' she had spent the rest of the day there. He took this as further proof she had submitted to the pressure he had exerted on her.

Finally, Khon'Tor stood up, and silence fell immediately. All heads turned to watch him stroll to the front. He did not signal for any of the others to join him. He did not want to give them another chance to usurp him, though he was confident they would not try it after this morning's meeting.

He raised his left hand as was his custom. A chill of foreboding ran through the crowd when they realized he was holding the Leader's Staff. Something of dire significance was about to take place.

"Thank you for joining me again so soon. For those of you who were in attendance yesterday afternoon, you are aware of what took place here. For those of you who were not, I am sure you have heard by now," he began.

"Adia, Healer of the People, has broken one of our Sacred Laws. For anyone to break a law is a serious offense. For someone to do it who is in a position of authority and respect as she is, makes it altogether more serious," continued the Leader.

"The laws were given to us by the Ancients for the orderly conduct and mutual benefit of our people. The First Laws are immutable and were established eons ago during the time of their rule. The Second Laws were added by later generations. They were also created for our mutual benefit, though they address the hierarchy of authority within our community, as well as establishing rules for personal relationships."

He was not stating anything they did not all know. He was only setting the stage for what he was about to declare.

"Adia, Healer of the People, has broken the law forbidding contact with Outsiders. More serious than breaking the statement of that law at its face value, she went further and brought an Outsider directly into our midst—a Waschini offspring. Yesterday, I shared with you information from the High Council meeting about the heartlessness of these creatures, and the threat the Waschini present to us and the Brothers. The Healer has explained the reasons for her actions, and what she asserts is true; as she has said, it is only an offspring."

"But though it is only an offspring and currently of little influence, it will grow. And as it grows, so will its skills, talents, and powers. And so will its influence. And along with that influence will come the ability to cause change brought out of its character and essence. Change that would not come about had it not been brought here to live among us."

"None of us knows the effect that bringing this offspring into our community will have on us in the long term—not even those so strongly connected to the Great Mother," continued Khon'Tor. As he spoke, he glanced in Adia's direction so everyone would know the comment was directed at her.

"But the act has been done. Regardless that this is a Waschini offspring, it is, as she says, an offspring nonetheless. And for that fact, recognizing that the role of the Healer is to protect and care for others, especially the weak or sick, or those in need, I will grant her some quarter for the crime she has committed."

Khon'Tor paused for a moment.

"Because Adia took it upon herself and acted alone in bringing the Waschini offspring here, it will be her responsibility to raise. It will be her burden alone. There will be no leniency; she will still be expected to fulfill her service completely as Healer to the People." At that statement, the crowd, which had until now been silent, broke into muted conversation.

Khon'Tor realized by their stirring that the severity of the Healer's sentence was not lost on his people.

An offspring was a tremendous responsibility and caring for one—perhaps even more so an Outsider offspring—would take a great deal of Adia's time and energy. Everyone there realized that in addition to the physical drain of caring for the offspring, Khon'Tor had created a massive internal conflict for her as well—she was expected to fulfill her role as Healer for the People without waiver. The second demand was, in truth, equally as crushing as the first.

Seeing the crowd's reaction, Khon'Tor quickly raised his hand as a signal for silence, and they complied.

"—for the most part," he added. He then called the four females of Adia's inner circle to come forward. While they were walking to the front, the talking within the crowd started again.

Once the females were standing next to him, he said, "I will allow two of these four females to help with the responsibilities of caring for the Waschini." Turning to address the four, but loudly enough that everyone could hear, he said, "You may decide among yourselves which two it will be." Giving them the choice was a concession on his part to the strain he was putting on their lives as well.

"In addition, the one who has been nursing the offspring, Pakuna, will be allowed to continue until it is weaned. At that point, her involvement will end."

For the moment, he let his people speak among themselves. The punishment was severe, but it could have been so much worse. Yesterday, Khon'Tor had stated that the offspring should be returned to where it was found and left to die. The People recognized that he had conceded a lot of ground from his original position. And as Leader, he did not have to give up any ground.

Khon'Tor felt his punishment was harsh but just. He had not ordered the offspring killed. He had not ordered Adia banished or stripped of her position. He had found a middle ground that, while it presented a great hardship to her, was not impossible. Her biggest problem was how she would juggle her responsibilities as Healer and as a *mother*.

There were good reasons why Healers were not allowed to pair and produce offspring—the risk of death while carrying and delivering an offspring was the often-stated consideration, but there was more. For Healers to meet the demands placed on them physically, mentally, and spiritually, time spent in self-care was critical. Time for solitude, rest, meditation, and regeneration—all these were crucial for a Healer's well-being. And caring for an offspring was conducive to none of it.

Khon'Tor continued with one final statement.

"I will say it clearly, however. If at any time the Waschini offspring presents a direct threat to this community, or to any member—*I will kill it myself.*"

No one moved; no one breathed.

Adia closed her eyes at his reiteration of this threat.

But it was not a threat.

It was a promise, and if it came to it, Khon'Tor would have no qualms in carrying it out.

Khon'Tor then turned to address the crimes of

his mate. Adia had violated a Second Law: No Contact With Outsiders. Though on face value Hakani's actions had been disrespectful to him as Leader and as her mate and had been in exceptionally poor taste, they were not necessarily a violation of any laws.

However, looking at the actions of both Adia and Hakani, his mate's crimes were far worse. If one considered the *impact* of her actions, Hakani had violated the *intent* of the first one of the First Laws, that personal actions and decisions be first and foremost in the best interests of the People, rather than for any personal interests or gain. But since Khon'Tor had still not figured out his mate's motives, he could not expect anyone else to, either.

In attacking Nadiwani, Hakani had also broken the First Law forbidding violence against another except in self-defense. And the People would understand that.

In truth, Khon'Tor was not sure he had the authority to revoke Hakani's rank, but he could not skirt over the severity of her crime. *I must do something to appease the community. Adia is revered, and if I do not address Hakani's actions, someone might appeal to the High Council.*

"Now, as to the actions of my mate—" He picked up the pace again, at which point everyone finally exhaled. The room fell into silence once more.

Though Hakani was standing against the wall opposite Adia and Nadiwani, she too was in plain sight. Khon'Tor intentionally refused to look in her direction as he began.

"—I make no excuses, nor will I offer any explanation for Hakani's actions. Because Hakani *is* my mate, you will have to accept my word that some of the repercussions for her behavior will be unknown to you but will be painful for her to bear. In abducting the Waschini from the Healer's Quarters, not only did she violate the sanctity of their space, but she also attacked the Healer's Helper, Nadiwani. Our law forbids violence against another except for self-defense.

"As for the public punishment of her crime, I now strip her of her position as Third Rank. She will no longer sit as one of the leadership, nor will she have any role of influence while I am Adik'Tar. Make no mistake; violence against each other will not be tolerated. And no one who attacks another has any right to hold a position of authority." As he spoke this last sentence, he looked across at Hakani.

The chill in his eyes conveyed not only the seriousness of Hakani's transgressions but also the weight of her punishment, declared and undeclared.

After the fiasco of yesterday, Khon'Tor was confident he had re-established himself as the unchallenged authority of the People of the High Rocks.

Having said all he had to say, and satisfied with the mindset of the crowd, Khon'Tor stood for a few seconds longer. Surveying the crowd one last time, instead of raising his arm as was his standard closing gesture, he raised and *slammed* the Leader's staff into the floor, the resounding *crack* signaling that an official decree had been issued.

Khon'Tor then stepped down from the front of the room. As he walked out, knowing all eyes were following him, he made sure he carried himself at his full height.

As soon as Khon'Tor exited, Adia and Nadiwani left as well. Hakani remained next to the side wall. The People filed past, not approaching her or looking in her direction. She felt invisible and humiliated and was seething inside. Khon'Tor had stripped her not only of her power; he had alluded to unknown punishments. And by not naming them, these were left to everyone's imagination.

She waited until nearly all had left the great hall and then sneaked to their quarters. When she walked in, she saw that in her absence, a separate bed had been set up across the room from the area she and Khon'Tor shared.

Hakani stood there horrified, her mouth hanging open. He did not do this himself. That means he ordered it done. *So others are now aware we no longer share the same bed? Has he exposed the intimate rift between us?*

Her public humiliation was complete.

Her satisfaction at finding a way to trump Adia's

power faded into the background. In her anger, she kicked at the arrangement of soft grasses and provisions, scattering them across the floor.

"That will do you no good, Hakani," came Khon'-Tor's voice from a corner of the room.

She spun around in shock. He was leaning against the wall, watching her; muscled arms crossed high on his chest.

Her anger welled up, and she lunged at him in a rage. Laughing, Khon'Tor easily caught both her wrists at once and pinned them in front of her, holding her defenseless.

"You are only making things worse, Hakani. I had the separate sleeping mat set up so you would not have to share mine. What you took as an insult was meant to be an accommodation to provide you some level of privacy."

She did not believe him. He surely did mean it as the insult she took it to be. It was his way of reminding her, *"When I want you, I will come to you, and other than that any other purpose you may have for me is dismissed."*

His arrogance enraged her. Even her earlier realization of the power that would come from bearing his offspring gave her no comfort. At the moment she wanted nothing more than to anger him, and she set aside her earlier concession to embrace the role of Asdza Ayashe Aama, Mother Of His Offspring.

"You may come begging to me all you wish,

Khon'Tor," she hissed, and spat at him. "I will never give my consent."

"Have it your way, Hakani," he replied calmly. "You may change your mind in time. If not, it is of no consequence to me. There are many willing young maidens eager to be mated by me and bear my offspring. I will give you some time to rethink your position, however."

Then he leaned forward and whispered in her ear, "Just do not take too long."

Still pinned, she was powerless to inflict on him the harm that she wished to. All she could do at the moment was to bare her teeth and hope he could read in her eyes how slowly and painfully she wanted to kill him, right then and there.

He added, "Oh, and I have also taken the liberty of having all sharp tools, objects, or anything else that could be used as a weapon removed from our quarters. Just to save you the time looking."

Adia and Nadiwani made it back to the Healer's Quarters together, and Acaraho positioned himself just outside the door. Though he knew no one could get past the guards he had stationed there, he still felt a need to be closer to the two females whom it was his duty to protect. With the situation as it was, Nadiwani would most likely be staying with Adia for the foreseeable future. It would be far easier to protect them both if they were sleeping under the same roof.

The day was finally over. After relaying to Donoma what had happened while she was watching over Oh'Dar, they both settled in for the evening. Confident of their safety with the presence of the massive Acaraho who insisted on staying just outside their door, and with Oh'Dar fast asleep, the two females themselves fell asleep very early. At least for a little while, they found peace from everything that had happened.

CHAPTER 9

The next morning, Adia and Nadiwani awoke and started discussing how they would care for Oh'Dar as well as fulfilling their duties to the People. Though it was Adia's burden, there was never a moment when Nadiwani did not stand with her in this responsibility.

Before they had been up too long, Acaraho announced that the females whom Khon'Tor had allowed to help were asking permission to enter.

"Of course," said Adia, curious as to which two it would be. "Please send them in."

Two of the original four females entered the room—Mapiya, who was the oldest of the original four, and Haiwee, who was the youngest. Mapiya had raised two offspring of her own, both males, and both of whom had already been paired and were established in their adult lives. Haiwee also had lots of experience and had more time to donate than the others because her son was nearly grown.

Adia was happy to see them and was filled with overwhelming gratitude for their help and their sacrifice. She hugged each of them. As she started to thank them, they both smiled and asked where the offspring was and if Adia had decided how they could best assist her in raising him.

Adia had no plan. She was still trying to catch up from yesterday. Nadiwani, however, did indeed have a plan. Not only did she have a plan, but she also had a schedule mapped out, as well as individual assignments. Once again, she had set aside her responsibilities and come to Adia's aid when the Healer needed her most.

As the four females sat down together, Nadiwani outlined the course of training she envisioned for the Waschini offspring.

"While he is an offspring, the matter of his care is relatively simple; keep him nourished, hydrated, safe, and warm. Of all those, the only one that presents a challenge is keeping him warm. Lacking our body hair, and given the constant cool temperature of the cave, the biggest risk for Oh'Dar is his core temperature dropping too low. So he has always to be encased in layers upon layers of wrappings. It is not a huge impediment since he is not mobile at present, but clearly, other arrangements will have to be made, and reasonably soon."

As she finished, an image popped suddenly into Nadiwani's mind: Is'Taqa standing next to Ogima Adoeete amid the chaos of the events of two nights before. She understood the message; the Brothers were also mostly hairless like the Waschini, and they were adept at fashioning warm wrappings out of tanned animal skins and hides. They would be able to supply whatever covering Oh'Dar needed. And since they had been there when Oh'Dar's presence was revealed, they were already aware of what Adia had done.

I am sure both Is'Taqa and his sister, the Brothers' Medicine Woman, would be glad to help. Khon'Tor said Adia could only have the help of two females from this community; he did not stipulate that there could be no help from outside the community.

Nadiwani next outlined the areas in which she believed Oh'Dar should be trained.

"First is Handspeak. We are unsure if he has the vocal capabilities to speak our language, so this is his best bet in joining our community." Handspeak was used commonly among the People and was the first language they taught their offspring.

Next on the list was the obvious; living with them he would learn about the natural medicines available through the plenty that surrounded them. Though Healer Helpers were traditionally females, there was no prohibition against males learning the trade. They lacked the seventh sense of the females, but they could still be of use in gathering and preparing the tinctures and powders in the Healer's pantry.

Down the road, he would need a male mentor; one who would eventually teach him the ways of hunting, preparation, fishing, toolmaking, and all that it meant to be a man. Who that might be was inconceivable at present. They filed it away for later; they did not need to resolve it now.

The last point on Nadiwani's list was controversial, to say the least. Though Khon'Tor had said Oh'Dar would never be allowed to leave and live among the Waschini, Nadiwani strongly felt that he should be taught their spoken language. Because she was not sure how Adia would feel about this, she did not share it in their little impromptu meeting. She thought it only fair to discuss it with Adia first; after all, the Healer was his mother.

Mother. Aama. Nadiwani wondered if this had even sunk in yet.

The other females stayed a while longer, then took their leave. Adia and Nadiwani still had much to discuss, and they were able to look after Oh'Dar themselves, for the time being, centering their activities within the Healer's Quarters and interrupted only by Pakuna's regular visits.

Because of the need not only for a sleeping area

but also for storage and preparation space, the Healer's Quarters were the largest private living space in the underground system. The best lit was the preparation area, into which the overhead tunnel allowed shafts of sunlight to enter. It did not provide a lot of light, but the People had better vision, and they were not hindered by low light conditions as were the Brothers.

Parallel to the back wall ran several long working platforms consisting of long, flat rock slabs. Though well beyond the ability of anyone with the strength of the Waschini or the Brothers, the males of the community had no problem at all moving rocks of that size. However, Adia had no memory of how the materials had been brought in; the Healer's Quarters had been set up long ago and were used by each Healer in succession. As with the modifications to the tunnels and Great Chamber, each generation of Healers had made improvements and modifications.

Overhead, behind the work platforms, hung rows and rows of herbs and grasses in various stages of drying. A multitude of hollowed-out gourds had also been hung from above and held the variety of powders, stems, and roots that Adia and Nadiwani used in their trade. Collections of dried flowers decorated the side walls—not because of their medicinal value but because they were beautiful and beauty was a gift of the Mother, to be incorporated inside Kthama wherever possible.

The People believed the soul needed at least

these five things to be healthy: gratitude, a sense of purpose and connection to the bigger picture of life, relationship with each other, humility, and to live in beauty.

At the farthest end of the quarters lay their sleeping arrangements. As Adia surveyed the area, she realized there was another problem. At present Oh'Dar was not very mobile, but that would change. As he gained the ability to move about, he would be into everything. She had to look with new eyes, foreseeing anything that might harm him, and remove or mitigate it.

Basing their estimates of his age on those of the Brothers' offspring they had seen, they believed he would be crawling soon. Nadiwani had already fashioned a Keeping Stone for him. Each member of each community had one. It was given at birth in the celebration ritual, something which Oh'Dar never had, and never would. The passage of time was marked on the stone, as well as special milestones in the offspring's life. A person's Keeping Stone was irreplaceable. As the offspring grew, a larger stone was used. When they returned to the Mother, the first Keeping Stone was placed with their remains or kept by the family as a remembrance that they had once walked among the People.

On the other side of the door, Acaraho heard all of this. The People had far better hearing than the Brothers and the Waschini.

Over the past few days, Adia and Nadiwani had seemed to be getting more and more comfortable with his presence. He wondered if they realized he could hear everything that went on in the Healer's Quarters.

Days passed into weeks. Nadiwani fashioned a sling in which to carry Oh'Dar around. *For being the spawn of the Waschini Monsters*, thought Adia, *Oh'Dar is remarkably calm and good-natured.*

Pakuna still came frequently to nurse him, and around all their other demands Adia and Nadiwani tended to their usual duties as Healers. No one went without care, but it was not easy.

For the most part; the tension between Adia and Khon'Tor had never subsided. Adia was very aware of it whenever she was in his presence, but she would not allow herself to be intimidated into being a prisoner in her quarters. She made a point of moving about the shared areas nearly every day. It was uncomfortable, but she knew if she allowed herself to retreat now, it would be even harder to resurface later.

Acaraho was still frequently assigned to protect

Adia, though as time passed, there were periods when he had to attend to other business. When Acaraho was not available, his First Guard, Awan, was at her side.

Though Acaraho was more than capable of helping her with her tasks, he only ever stood near her. He never offered, nor did she ask for anything more. Aware of his position as High Protector, Adia was grateful for his presence. She had heard many stories of his great skill and bravery. She could relax, knowing that with him at their sides, they were as safe as anyone could possibly be.

Adia still considered Hakani a threat to Oh'Dar, and always would. She shuddered, remembering how Hakani had hoisted Oh'Dar up over her head. *How easily she could have lost control; a fall from that height onto the hard rock floor of the cave would have killed him for sure.* She could also not rule out some aberrant element that might side with Hakani in seeing the Waschini offspring as a threat.

So Adia accepted Acaraho's presence and did not try to alter the arrangement. She also did not try to enter into conversation with Acaraho or interact with him in any other way. A second guard was still always posted outside the tunnel to her quarters, in accordance with Khon'Tor's original command. This left someone always in place when Acaraho followed her on her errands.

I still have not found a way to get word to Ithua or Is'Taqa about borrowing warm wrappings for Oh'Dar.

*The weather will be turning cold soon. Oh'Dar will
become more mobile, and his cumbersome wad of coverings will become an impediment.*

Adia could still feel Khon'Tor's anger smoldering
underneath the surface. The last thing she wanted to
do was to fan the fire. But time was ticking by, and
she needed to make arrangements for sufficient
wrappings to keep Oh'Dar warm while accommo-
dating his increasing mobility.

Letting out a deep sigh, Adia accepted that she
needed to approach Khon'Tor directly.

Adia realized that no matter how angry Khon'Tor
had been with her—and still was—his wrath against
Hakani was much greater.

Though they had never been openly affectionate,
or in retrospect that friendly either, the physical
distance between Khon'Tor and Hakani was now
even more considerable. They made no eye contact
with each other, and Hakani acted more submis-
sively around Khon'Tor—more like a stranger would
act than a mate. There were rumors of separate
sleeping arrangements. As Hakani was no longer
preparing food for him since the incident with
Oh'Dar, Khon'Tor had started taking his meals in the
Great Chamber with the community.

So, when she saw an opening, Adia slowly
approached Khon'Tor, purposefully giving him time

to realize she was coming to speak with him. He scowled, and his eyes seemed to bore holes in her as she approached. She almost had to look away.

"I need to speak with you, Khon'Tor," Adia said. Khon'Tor silently nodded his agreement.

"The offspring is becoming more mobile. Soon he will be crawling about. Kthama is too cold for him, and I need more versatile wrappings to keep him warm," she explained.

He said nothing, only staring at her blankly. He then went back to his meal, leaving her standing there.

She continued, "I wish to borrow warmer wrappings for him from the Brothers. Is'Taqa and Ogima Adoeete were present when Hakani—" Her words trailed off.

Khon'Tor sighed and looked her up and down before replying. "I will allow it." And he turned his attention away—cutting off any further conversation and letting her know she had been dismissed.

Khon'Tor was confident he had clearly conveyed that he had no interest in the offspring or whatever difficulties she might encounter in providing for it.

But the truth and what he intended to convey were two different matters. Khon'Tor had been getting updates from Acaraho about the two females and the offspring.

When Khon'Tor had assigned Acaraho to protect Adia, that was as far as he intended it to go. However, Acaraho was, by default of his assignment, now privy to what was taking place with Adia, the others, and the offspring. Khon'Tor soon realized he could use Acaraho's knowledge to his advantage.

As Adia walked away, and as soon as Khon'Tor knew she would not look back in his direction, he lifted his head and watched her leave—for an indulgent moment admitting how beautiful he still found her to be. Usually, when Khon'Tor felt his attraction for Adia rise within him, he squashed it immediately. He had become accustomed to his anger toward her. It had almost become a comfort. As long as he was angry with Adia, his relationship with her was clearly defined. Having a singular reaction to her greatly uncomplicated her constant presence.

As far as his relationship with Hakani went, that had settled into one of outright mutual disdain and avoidance. When one of them was in their quarters, the other made sure not to be. They avoided eye contact when they were in public together. He never invited her to sit or stand at his side. For Khon'Tor's part, his actions were a continued, intentional statement of his dismissal of her from his life in any capacity—except the one he had made clear was her obligation to fulfill.

Though he was never at risk from her physically, the level of hatred she evidenced toward him left its impression. A male of the People was never justified in hitting a female; in fact, it was punishable under one of the laws. But he was allowed to defend himself if she initiated the attack, using the least amount of force necessary. However, even with that, he had no fear of her in a direct one-on-one confrontation between them. She was no match for him by any means. But she was clever, and he did not put it past her to take revenge on him at some point through some indirect manipulation or scheme. Khon'Tor could tell that Hakani was still intent on refusing to provide him with offspring—or even trying to do so.

I do not want to approach the High Council and let the other Leaders know that a female refuses me. But allowing them to believe she is simply infertile does not guarantee that they would let me move Hakani to separate quarters. And having two females under one roof, one of which expressly hates me, and the other of which would be jealous? No, thank you. But if it comes to that, I shall. I will not put up forever with her refusal to mate with me.

Though they did not know the specifics, the People were aware of the tension between the three Leaders. Khon'Tor was at war with the two females with whom he had primary relationships—his mate and the People's Healer.

Adia's mind was taxed by the many challenges she faced. It was only at night, lying in the quiet, uninterrupted peace of the dark, that she allowed her feelings to surface.

She realized that what she had done had changed the community forever. The members of the general population were no longer able to focus solely on their own business. The overriding tension between the three Leaders, and curiosity and concern over the presence of the Waschini offspring and what it might mean to the futures of them all had taken its toll on their previously peaceful existence.

Adia's actions had changed the interaction between the three of them. *We never did have an easy relationship. But at least whatever tension existed between Khon'Tor and me was manageable. But now we are openly at odds. And whatever grudge Hakani holds against me has only deepened. She openly bristles now when I am around.*

In the past, it was only Khon'Tor and his mate who had negative feelings toward her. Now, however, Adia struggled with her anger and resentment of them. She could never let herself forget Hakani's utter disregard for Oh'Dar's safety, nor the continued threat that Adia was confident Hakani still presented to the offspring and to her.

Thinking of this, Adia gave thanks again for Acaraho's continual presence. She was not afraid of Hakani. She was afraid of what she would do to

Hakani in a second altercation. Acaraho's presence prevented that opportunity from arising.

Adia wondered how Khon'Tor might have reacted had Hakani not inflamed the problem of Oh'Dar by revealing his presence in such an incendiary display.

She spoke into the dark, *"I miss you, Father. You were such a strong yet gentle Leader. You never ruled with a clenched fist. You respected the laws, but you did not wield them like a weapon. I wish you could tell me how to live in peace with Khon'Tor. I cannot understand his strong-armed approach."*

Then again, she wondered if she was unfair; she knew her father had been a rare combination of wisdom, kindness, and strength. She doubted any of the People would ever see the likes of that kind of leadership again.

Adia then remembered she *had* wanted to go to Khon'Tor in private. But when he had told them of the High Council's warning about the Waschini, she decided the time was not right.

Adia tossed and turned, unable to sleep. The night afforded her the only privacy she had, and finally, she let the tears come. *What if Khon'Tor is right. What if Oh'Dar never does fit in? What if he never finds a real place here, never finds a mate? Is that what I rescued him for? To live as an outcast? The last thing I want is for him to live like me, alone at night with no one to share my burdens—no one to turn to for comfort, support, and affection.*

Every night, just before sleep finally came, Adia would remind herself of the promise she had received, that ultimately this would all work for the good of her people and Oh'Dar, and she focused on surrendering her fears.

CHAPTER 10

One day turned into another, and another. Nadiwani was making great progress in teaching Handspeak to Oh'Dar. Like the offspring of the People, he was able to learn the meanings before he had the motor skills to sign back. He had learned the basics—eat, water, sleep, more, done, pick me up, Mama. He used the sign for Mama interchangeably between Nadiwani and Adia. It did not bother Adia that he also considered Nadiwani to be his mother. She knew he needed all the love he could get if he were to find a place in this world. This world into which she had delivered him.

Word of the Outsiders continued to trickle in, but there was no mention of the need to invoke Wrak-Ayya, though what they learned about the Waschini did nothing to ease concerns. What the Waschini lacked in physical strength, they made up for in ingenuity. Like the Brothers, they took the resources the

Great Spirit provided and modified them to their own use. The People also did this but to a different extent. And while the People and the Brothers were content to live in harmony with the Great Spirit, the Waschini seemed intent on bullying her into submission to their uses and designs.

Adia grew uncomfortable with Acaraho's station outside the door and started to invite him into the interior of her quarters. Though he still stood guard in front of the door, from this vantage point he had even more detailed information on the offspring's progress to give to Khon'Tor. Though he tried to maintain objectivity, his respect for Adia continued to grow with his first-hand knowledge of the burden she was shouldering with such dignity and grace.

Though she suspected Acaraho might be passing news on to Khon'Tor, Adia did not fault him for it. Neither did she see it as negative. She hoped Acaraho was telling him about more than Oh'Dar's developmental progress, but about the offspring himself. *Does Acaraho notice Oh'Dar's sweet disposition, his quickness to laugh, and the delight he takes in the simplest of things? He is fascinated by the plants and minerals that make up his world here. He is inquisitive and bright. If there is a monster lurking inside him, I can see no evidence of it.*

She wondered if Acaraho was sensitive enough to notice these qualities and was also making Khon'Tor aware of them.

Through the information coming in about the

Waschini, Adia learned that her people lived longer, though they seemed to reach maturity about the same time. From that standpoint, she was able to compare Oh'Dar's development to the community offspring of his approximate age. Compared to his counterparts, Oh'Dar fell far behind in size and strength.

The People's offspring were easily twice his size at the same age. They were already walking, picking up items, getting into everything. Oh'Dar was starting to walk, but he was shaky and often fell over. His build was not as robust as theirs. Even without Khon'Tor's restrictions, Oh'Dar could not play with the other offspring. The differences would put him at immediate risk of serious injury or even death.

When it came to intellectual development, Oh'Dar was keeping pace with the others. He had the same inquisitiveness and the same ability to learn new signs. He seemed to be more innovative, making constructions of the items he played with in a way that the Sasquatch offspring never did. Compared to theirs, his manual dexterity was superior—perhaps attributable to his smaller and more delicate hands and fingers? Adia was not sure of that, but taking the different builds out of the picture, he did seem to have finer control of his hand and finger movements.

Adia took these differences as neither good nor bad and noted them only for consideration as he developed, looking for ways in which these differences might be turned into attributes and not detriments. Khon'Tor had issued a challenge when he declared the offspring would never be a contributing member of the community. Adia would find a place for him, but it could not be a decision made from her will and must come naturally out of Oh'Dar's own gifts. Adia knew that for Oh'Dar to have any chance at satisfaction in his life, he would have to find his place here among the People.

Adia was also aware that the more he grew, the smaller his world here in her quarters would become.

Making blathering noises, Oh'Dar grinned up at Adia. She smiled at him, knowing this was the precursor to speech; he was learning the sounds and structure of language.

"Whose smart boy is that? Yes, you are starting to understand me, aren't you?"

Nadiwani came over to them, "I still think he needs to learn Whitespeak. I know there are risks, but there are also benefits."

"I know. And we are not any further toward making a decision. Is Khon'Tor right? Can Oh'Dar never be returned to the Waschini world? Not even as an adult?" Adia asked, not expecting an answer.

And if he does learn Whitespeak, what would be the benefit? Unless he leaves the People and goes to live among the Waschini, there seems no point in his learning it. Having been raised among the People, would he be less of an Outsider among the White Men? But she could not shake the feeling that it was important he learn the Waschini language.

Nadiwani pointed out to Adia, "The window of opportunity will close at some point. Now starts the critical stage when offspring seem to have the greatest capacity to learn language. He might even be able to learn *both* languages; we do not know the limits to his abilities. And even we cannot see every possible outcome and twist or turn the future might bring for him."

"I agree. And like it or not, the boy is Waschini. I do not have the right to close the door on his heritage. I have at least to give him the chance to learn his native language. But where will we find a Whitespeak teacher?"

☾

Before Acaraho came off duty, he always met with his First Guard, Awan, and the other guards and watchers. Then he would return to his quarters, the only place where he could drop his guard altogether. Like all the other single quarters, it had a small sleeping area off to the side, a food preparation area, storage, seating, and an area for personal care. He did much of his thinking and reflection when his long, muscular frame was stretched out at night on the filled sleeping mat.

If he was uncomfortable in his developing role between the Leader and the Healer, he never expressed it. He understood Khon'Tor's need to know what was going on with the offspring. The High Protector remembered Khon'Tor's statement that if the offspring ever presented a threat, he would kill it himself. Acaraho never doubted Khon'Tor would follow through on his threat and do exactly as he had said.

Acaraho was now privy to the world of the two females nearly every waking moment. But he had never participated. He was there to provide protection for them and the offspring; he was there to provide information for Khon'Tor. He was not there to take part in any way. So, when they were talking about the need for a Whitespeak teacher, Acaraho found himself in a difficult situation.

For one thing, Acaraho knew Adia was right— *If Khon'Tor learns that they are even considering giving Oh'Dar the chance to learn Whitespeak, he will be very angry. Khon'Tor is already convinced the offspring presents a threat—in his mind, it is just a matter of time before that materializes. Adding anything that increases the offspring's connection with the Waschini also increases the risk to the People.*

However, Acaraho's dilemma was not about Khon'Tor's reaction to this latest development but something else. Acaraho had the solution to their problem.

I know where to find a Whitespeak teacher for the Waschini offspring. I have been able to remain neutral so far, but now that I see how they love the boy, how gentle and kind they are with him, I am not sure I can remain impartial. The Healer is exhausted, yet she presses on. She pushes herself to bear up under the burden Khon'Tor has placed on her to fill without leeway the roles of both Healer and mother.

Acaraho's respect for Nadiwani and even more for Adia had grown with each additional day he spent in their company.

Acaraho was losing his neutrality.

❂

Though Khon'Tor was indeed a master strategist, his shortcomings blindsided him to the risk he had created in placing Acaraho in such close interaction with the females and the offspring. Khon'Tor was ruled by his will; he forgot that not everyone else was.

Acaraho and Khon'Tor shared many similarities. Both were very intelligent, both were in positions of great authority and leadership in the community, both possessed exceptional physical attributes. In a contest of sheer strength, the victor would be the one who executed the better strategy or the one who had more to lose because they were otherwise so well-matched.

But where Khon'Tor was very protective of his position of authority and was driven to maintain it at whatever cost, Acaraho did not *have* to be the one in charge. He possessed a strong will; he achieved whatever he set his mind to. But he was not driven by a desire to be the one in control.

Khon'Tor, on the other hand, was so consumed by his need to be in command that his will overruled any input from his other faculties. In a struggle between his heart and his head, Khon'Tor would subjugate his heart without hesitation. Power was so important to Khon'Tor that he could not conceive of anyone else in authority voluntarily risking their position for anything. It would never occur to Khon'Tor that Acaraho might put his high level of power in jeopardy based on the leading of his heart.

It was not that Acaraho had romantic feelings for either of the females. He knew their positions prevented it; plus he knew it was a complication he did not need to entertain. But he respected them and discovered he cared about them. He found their quest honorable and admired the integrity with which they pursued it.

He could have done nothing. But he would have had to betray his conscience as well as these females of whom he thought so highly, and he had to live with himself.

So Acaraho stepped down from his neutral position and decided to do whatever was within his power to help Adia, Nadiwani, and Oh'Dar—even if it came at his detriment.

Acaraho had no intention of falling on his sword. He knew he needed to get to them the information he possessed about the teacher for Oh'Dar, but had to figure out a way to do so without tipping his hand. If he wanted to continue helping them, he could best do so by maintaining his position as their protector and his role as informant to Khon'Tor. *Khon'Tor has no interest in what would benefit the offspring; Khon'Tor cares only about what would benefit Khon'Tor. Somehow, I have to make Khon'Tor want Oh'Dar to learn Whitespeak.*

CHAPTER 11

While events were calming down for Adia, Nadawani, and the offspring, they were not going so well for Khon'Tor.

His life had gotten immeasurably worse. He was saddled with a mate who no longer secretly hated him but now openly and actively expressed it, who still refused to receive him to provide an heir to his leadership, who was effectively calling his bluff of going to the High Council and asking for a second mate. Because of her presence, there was no peace in his quarters. And now there was peace nowhere else either because wherever he went, he was reminded of Adia.

Khon'Tor noticed that when Adia took her walks outside others stopped and spoke with her—the males as well as the females. Khon'Tor knew the favor of the entire community was turning toward her. And the more Adia's popularity grew, the more Khon'Tor's hatred of her also grew. In spite of his efforts to crush her, she had risen up even stronger.

How quickly they have forgiven her, despite the seriousness of what she did. She broke the laws. She openly challenged my authority. And she brought a tremendous threat directly into our midst. This is not justice; none of this is justice.

The offspring is growing. And as it grows, so will its skills and abilities and powers. And so will its influence. According to Acaraho, it has proven adept at learning Handspeak. It will not be long before it is able to converse with others of my people. And the odds are it will endear itself to everyone, in the same way it has charmed those now close to it.

Khon'Tor did not know how to turn the tide against them, so he was waiting either for an opportunity to present itself or until he could create one.

Any other Leader would not have cared about any of this. Any other Leader would have seen this as a good turn of events—unity was being brought back to the People of the High Rocks. The drama of what had taken place had subsided. Everyone, including Adia and Nadiwani, was returning to their normal lives. Any other Leader would have welcomed this outcome, would not have resented the favor the Healer and the offspring were winning from the People. Any other Leader except one as consumed with power as Khon'Tor. But just at the point when he did not think he could live with it for another minute, a golden opportunity dropped right into his lap.

Acaraho did not forget his dilemma over helping Adia find a Whitespeak teacher for Oh'Dar. He hesitated at the time because he was afraid Khon'Tor might be able to use it to turn the People against her. But now, seeing how fully she had won the hearts of the community, he was confident her favor could take a hit from any backlash Khon'Tor might be able to stir up against her.

The High Protector did not acknowledge that Khon'Tor resented, or even hated Adia. Instead, he always delivered his report as if Khon'Tor would be glad to hear how well she was doing.

When the two met, they discussed general community business. Technically, both Adia and Hakani outranked Acaraho, but functionally he was higher in authority as he commanded the tasks of the other males. He was effectively in the position of authority closest to that of Khon'Tor, and he also had far greater influence over the Leader than either Adia or Hakani had.

Khon'Tor had called Acaraho for a report on what new was taking place, if anything, and was seated in front of Acaraho in one of the small meeting rooms, his chin on his hands and a foul look on his face. He got right to the point at hand. "What is the latest news? Have there been any developments with the Healer or the Waschini?"

Acaraho gave the standard report of the offspring's progress—how he was developing, his continued good relationship with Adia and Nadi-wani, what he was expressing interest in, the fact that his Handspeak skills were progressing remarkably well.

Khon'Tor nodded his head blandly in acknowledgment.

When Acaraho finished, the Leader thanked him and bade him goodnight. Then, before leaving, Acaraho turned back to face Khon'Tor.

"Oh," he said. "There is one other thing," he looked to make sure he had Khon'Tor's full attention.

"As you remember, the offspring is learning our language. But there is something more you should know. The Healer wants to find a Whitespeak teacher for him so he can learn the Waschini language."

Khon'Tor lifted his head, a puzzled look on his face. Knowing him, Acaraho was aware that Khon'Tor was trying to figure out if this was good or bad for himself. With Acaraho's next statement, he led Khon'Tor exactly where he wanted the Leader to go.

"Things are quieting down among the People.

The drama has fallen from their memory. Those community members who of necessity have come in contact with the offspring seem to have accepted him as one of our own. I fear if the Waschini learns Whitespeak, it might be too much a reminder of his true heritage, and it might turn them against him. If she is not careful, the Healer might lose all the gains she has made in finding acceptance for him."

Khon'Tor smiled. Here was the opportunity he needed—a chance to turn opinion back against her.

It was difficult for Adia to have Acaraho around and keep ignoring him. She was kind-hearted and felt it disrespectful to overlook his presence, never including him in conversation, treating him as if he was just another object in the room. And so, over time, she inched the line a little further forward, acknowledging him as a person instead of merely a bodyguard.

She started by addressing Acaraho by his name. The first time she did it, she worried that she was behaving too familiarly toward him. But she had to start somewhere, and a name was about as basic as you could get. He did not correct her or signal in any way that she was acting inappropriately. She started simply, thanking him, or using his name in welcoming him. He never made eye contact with her, though she sometimes caught him appraising her just as she looked away.

Over time, she started giving him small things to do—asking him to hand her down a basket or giving him something to hold for her for a moment. He never objected, seeming to welcome the overtures. But not in public. In public, she never treated him as anything other than the High Protector.

Maybe I should not blur the lines, she thought. *But I cannot treat Acaraho as if he does not exist. He has been part of our daily lives now for some time. He has listened to all our plans and conversations. He was here when Oh'Dar made his first sign for Mama; when he took his first steps. Maybe it's partly my loneliness too. I know he's seen me with tears in my eyes.*

How odd, this stranger about whom I know nothing probably knows me better than anyone else except Nadiwani.

One morning Adia and Nadiwani were sitting across from each other lost in their conversation, having forgotten Acaraho was present.

"Oh'Dar is doing so well. He is even starting to say some of our words, though he cannot quite get the hang of it yet," said Nadiwani.

"I know. I try not to laugh, but it is so comical."

"Me too. He is so bright, Adia. He soaks up everything we give him."

"I cannot shake it. My mind tells me there might never be a need for him to speak the Waschini language, and that in doing so I might be sending him a message that he should at some point try to return to them. Even raising it might anger Khon'Tor to the extent that he makes it even harder on us, though I am not sure how he could do that, as difficult as things already are. But no matter what my reason tells me, in my heart, I feel it is the right path for Oh'Dar." Adia shook her head and then rested her chin in her hands. When she looked up again, tears were streaming down her face.

"I do not know what to do. I am so torn, Nadiwani. My heart is breaking for fear of making the wrong decision."

Nadiwani reached out and took her friend's hand.

"Adia." A male's voice broke the silence.

Adia peered backward at the only male in the room.

She was afraid to move, as if a butterfly had just landed on her hand, and any movement would scare it away.

Acaraho took a step toward them. "Forgive my interruption. I realize it is an aberration from my assignment to speak to you directly. I hope you will forgive the transgression."

Adia could not remember if she had ever heard his voice before. It was deep and low, rich and comforting. The strength of his soul shining through his eyes kept her gaze locked on his.

She swallowed hard, "Please; please go on." If Acaraho was tall when she was standing next to him, he was a giant looming over them as they sat.

"It is not my place to counsel you. If you wish to make a report to Khon'Tor for my doing so, that is your right. But I have been a witness to your continued struggle over this particular matter, and I feel I must speak up at this time," he said.

"It has been my responsibility and my honor to protect you these past few months. Know I could have refused this appointment had I wished, but I have accepted it willingly. I say this to assure you I mean to bring you no harm in what I am about to say."

Adia and Nadiwani continued to stare up at him, unblinking, like rabbits caught in the stare of a predator, unable to move.

"You are standing at a crossroads and time is running out. If you fail to decide whether or not the offspring should learn Whitespeak, the decision will be made by default."

Adia regained her ability to blink. His wisdom registered with her deeply. She was losing time with her indecision. One way or the other, she needed to pick a direction.

And then, just when they thought he was done speaking, he leaned toward Adia slightly and said, "I have seen you do far braver things than this, Adia."

She inhaled sharply at this second use of her name.

Acaraho returned to standing against the wall, by which she knew he was signaling a return to their earlier rules of engagement. She felt a wave of sadness come over her that he had stepped back over the line he had just crossed. A window had opened and then closed.

Nadiwani looked at Adia and Adia looked at Nadiwani. It was time to go to Khon'Tor.

For the second day in a row, providence smiled on the Leader.

After the evening meal, he was seated in his usual secluded spot in the Great Chamber. Again, Hakani was nowhere to be found. Adia approached him much as she had done previously when she asked him about the wrappings for Oh'Dar.

And just as he had before, Khon'Tor received her with an icy silence. But this time he spoke first as she sat down next to him. "Another favor, Adia?" he asked her.

Khon'Tor had no clue what this was about, but he did not have time for it. He was still trying to figure out how to broach the idea of the offspring learning Whitespeak without Adia knowing that he knew about it through Acaraho. He could think of absolutely no platform from which to launch the suggestion.

Thinking that with the colder weather approaching, she was coming to ask again about the wrappings for Oh'Dar, he brought it up himself in an effort to end the conversation.

"If you are here to ask again about the wrappings for the Waschini offspring, I have word that Is'Taqa himself will be bringing them shortly, perhaps as early as in the next few days. Make sure you are prepared to receive them," he said, meaning she should have her reciprocal gifts ready.

"Thank you, Khon'Tor. I appreciate knowing this, but that is not the reason I am here. You have made it clear the offspring is my responsibility alone, and I hope you can acknowledge that I have fully shouldered this responsibility up until now. However, I am at a point where I need to ask for your help with a fundamental issue in which time is of the essence," she continued.

Khon'Tor started to take interest. *Again, Adia is about to ask for my help with something important.*

He saw an opportunity open to enjoy himself at her expense. He could hardly wait for the pleasure of her reaction when he coldly refused her request, whatever it was. In presenting him an opportunity to inflict a level of suffering on her, however slight, she now had his full attention.

"I am sure you know there is a window of opportunity in an offspring's development during which they have the aptitude for learning a language. He is learning to understand our language, though I believe that differing physical structure means he will speak with the same accent as do the Brothers." She paused so he could ask a question if he wished.

Khon'Tor's attention sharpened. Wherever she was going with this, he might be able to turn it in the direction he wanted regarding Whitespeak.

Adia spoke again. "I ask that you give my next request serious consideration before you reply. I am aware your reaction may well be negative, but it is of such importance that I am willing to risk it."

She took a controlled breath before continuing. "I would like permission for the offspring to be taught his native language while there is still opportunity," she said.

Khon'Tor could not quite believe what he was hearing. Here he was struggling with the problem of how to raise the subject with her when she comes to him and brings it up herself. And because Adia had asked, she would be indebted to him if he granted it.

Khon'Tor had every intention of granting her request, but she did not know that. He saw an opportunity to leverage the moment by exacting a debt in return for graciously helping her out. *For her to come to me and ask for this, she must want it very badly.*

"You want permission to train that Waschini in the language of its barbaric people?" he asked, knitting his brows together in disapproval. He was not sure exactly how long he would drag this out, but he wanted to see her squirm.

It was not a question needing a response, so Adia said nothing.

"And why should I help you in this regard, Adia?" he scoffed. "Of what possible benefit is it to me to help you *or* the Waschini?"

Adia had no answer, and Khon'Tor sneered as she shifted and looked at him blankly. He knew his cold glare was making her uncomfortable, and he was enjoying every minute of it.

He paused to let the pressure between them build before continuing. When he spoke again, he did so very deliberately and with measured cadence. He leaned intimidatingly toward her. *Let's see how badly she wants it.*

"If I grant you this, you will owe me a debt that must be repaid when called. I will not know what the debt is until the time comes to ask for it. When I require that you repay this obligation, you must do so," he said.

"Whatever is required of you to fulfill your part of this agreement, I give you my word it will not involve inflicting harm or allowing harm to come to another. But when I ask for it, if you do not comply then either your life or the life of that offspring will be forfeit to me to do with as I will. The choice of which one I will leave up to you at that time."

Then he sat back and waited.

The tension between them seemed to shoot up and bounce off the rocky ceiling. Everyone in the room was watching by now, knowing something momentous was taking place. Acaraho stood off to the side, transfixed.

Adia sat in motionless silence with downcast eyes, and Khon'Tor worried that he had perhaps overplayed his hand. He knew what he was extracting was unfair compared to what he was granting. He might just have lost his opportunity to give her exactly what he wanted her to have—for the offspring to be taught Whitespeak. But, as an indicator of how badly she wanted it, he was counting on how difficult it must have been for her to approach him in the first place.

Khon'Tor waited as the moments passed, making sure his breathing was controlled and slow, unclenching his jaw and his shoulders; not willing to convey his almost unbearable tension in waiting for her response.

She finally lifted her eyes and spoke.

"The deal is unfair. It is not enough that you grant permission for the offspring to learn Whitespeak; you must also provide a way for it to be accomplished. You must provide the Teacher," she counter-offered.

Khon'Tor almost let out a loud sigh of relief but caught himself.

He knew he now had the upper hand. By making the counteroffer, Adia had given him the winning move. All he had to do was agree, and the deal was struck. Adia would owe him a debt, the nature and timing of which would be of his choosing and solely under his control. If she fulfilled it, he got what he wanted—whatever that would be. If she did not fulfill it, he still won—perhaps even more so, because if she failed to meet his demand, he would gain ultimate power over her. He knew she would never forfeit the offspring's life but would forfeit hers instead. He would finally have the control over her that he had wanted for so long.

Using every ounce of his will to hide his excitement, Khon'Tor looked her squarely in the eye and said, "It is done then. The deal has been agreed to by both parties."

With that, he held up his left hand, palm facing Adia, his eyes still locked on hers. All those watching knew full well what this signified.

It was the highest agreement that could be made between two People—an agreement from which neither party could withdraw. The rules of the agreement were strict, and the consequences for breaking it were so severe that it was reserved only for the most critical issues; the most solemn occasions. It signified a commitment of great importance—an irrevocable and unbreakable vow.

It was the Rah-hora, a sacred obligation of honor among the People.

The room was in total silence; everyone was transfixed on the scene before them as they waited, Khon'Tor's hand still raised, his palm facing Adia.

Never blinking or taking her eyes off his, Adia raised her hand. She had only heard of the Rah-hora. She had never witnessed it done before, but she knew what was required. However, instead of just placing her palm against his as the ritual required, she slammed it against his. A loud, resounding *crack* split the silence and echoed throughout the chamber.

It was done. The agreement was sealed.

Even when I've beaten her, Adia will not stay down, thought Khon'Tor—only he used a very derogatory term in place of her name. *No matter her little show of rebellion. I have won, and more importantly, she also knows I have won. Let her continue her defiance. It will only make my ultimate victory over her that much sweeter.*

Adia dug her nails into her thighs. This was a tremendous price to extract. He had forced her to agree to pay an unidentified debt of his choosing, solicited at the time of his choosing. If she did not fulfill that debt, her life or that of her offspring would be placed in his hands to do with as he wished.

Adia knew that by *forfeit,* he did not mean he would have the right to kill one of them. She knew that was far outside the laws, and as much as he hated her, Khon'Tor would never go that far. She knew it to mean he would have complete authority over the state and condition of the life of either her or Oh'Dar. Not servitude, but a state of domination in which he would make choices for them without opportunity for consent or objection, and with which they must comply. If there was a worse fate than to be at his mercy, she could not imagine it.

Adia was angry. She knew he had backed her into a corner. Had she and Nadiwani not both had such an overpowering feeling about the importance of this for Oh'Dar, she would never have taken the deal. She had just given him enormous hold over her.

She squared her shoulders and rose to leave. Despite her fear, she could not help but deliver one last act of defiance. "Remember, Khon'Tor. Time is of the essence. If you do not hold up your end of the agreement, I am not obligated to honor mine."

And then she turned and walked away, feeling she had just forfeited her soul to the male who hated her with such a vengeance.

She asked herself, *What have I done?*

In the back of the room, Acaraho had watched it all unfold. Despite the acoustics, he could not hear the conversation. But he could read their body language, and it was obvious Khon'Tor had the upper hand and was using it to his full advantage. He had never seen Adia so uncomfortable. Confident that he knew why Adia had approached Khon'Tor and for what she had asked, he thought Khon'Tor would simply agree immediately to her request, seeing it as a means by which to turn the People's favor against her. He had not thought the Leader would leverage the moment to add another advantage.

I underestimated Khon'Tor. Acaraho made a vow never to let that happen again.

When he saw Khon'Tor raise his hand with his palm outfacing, he knew the Leader was initiating Rah-hora. With all his strength, knowing how much Khon'Tor wanted Adia destroyed, Acaraho urgently willed her not to raise her hand.

"Do not do it, please, whatever it is, do not take the deal."

When Adia's palm connected with Khon'Tor's, the sound pierced his heart.

Whatever agreement they had made, it was irrevocable. It was Rah-hora. Realizing the role he had played in creating the scenario he had just witnessed in motion, he also asked himself, *What have I done?*

As Adia left the room, Acaraho fell in behind her, never forgetting his responsibility to her as her protector. They walked in silence, as was usual, only this time each was internally actively struggling with what had taken place.

Adia believed with all her heart that learning Whitespeak was somehow critical to Oh'Dar's future. But now, not knowing what price Khon'Tor might extract from her was a burden almost heavier than she could bear. She had never felt more alone. And there was no one she could turn to for counsel.

The nature of the Rah-hora was that no one but the two parties could know what the agreement was. The only way in which the Rah-hora could be broken was for the initiating party to fail to fulfill their end, to release the other voluntarily, or for either party to break confidence and reveal the details. Adia knew there was no way Khon'Tor would default now that he had the upper hand. Sick at heart, she realized he had her exactly where he wanted her.

Khon'Tor was still sitting in the gathering room, congratulating himself on his victory. *I did not even have to work for it—it was delivered directly into my hands, so to speak. It would have been binding enough, the spoken agreement between us, but I have to admit that initiating the Rah-hora was a stroke of genius.*

Though he did not know when and where he would call her debt due, he relished the thought. Just as the details of the agreement were secret, so were the details of how and when payment was collected, both before and after the event. The parties were never to speak of any of it to anyone.

Picturing how it might play out would keep him up at night for a long time to come.

The Leader finally rose and headed to his quarters. *I have not seen Hakani all night. She was not here when I initiated the Rah-hora with Adia.* Khon'Tor smiled. *She is going to be so disappointed when she hears what she missed.*

Hakani and Adia were the two thorns in Khon'-Tor's side, each refusing to stay down after they were beaten, both challenging him publicly. They were in positions of authority under him and should have been complying with his will, not fighting it. Somehow, they were becoming merged in his mind, his anger at each spilling over to the other.

Khon'Tor was so elated that he did not care if Hakani was in their shared quarters when he got there. Nothing could dampen his victory of finally winning control over Adia.

Hakani was indeed in their quarters when Khon'Tor entered. They had spent so much time carefully avoiding each other that it caught her off guard when he appeared. Fully expecting him to take one look at her, abruptly turn his back as a gesture of dismissal and then leave, she was disconcerted when he did neither.

Why is he in such a good mood? He does not deserve any happiness or pleasure. The fact that Khon'Tor was apparently enjoying himself over something was the last thing she wanted to see.

Whereas Khon'Tor would have avoided her a few

hours before, he now walked in front of her, on the way cutting too close into her personal space.

From how he was acting, it seemed to Hakani that Khon'Tor was returning their relationship—that currently consisted of distance and evasion—back to battle state.

Their orchestrated avoidance of each other had created a rest period for Hakani. She used the time to reassess her goals. The only pleasure in her life was the thought of inflicting pain on her mate and the Healer; it seemed her life had no purpose other than to cause them trouble. Hakani had resigned herself to the stalemate with Khon'Tor, but if he was reviving the fight between them, she was more than willing to hold up her end.

There is nothing else he can do to me. He has taken away every role I had except the one I do not want—to bear his offspring. The community has turned against me because of that Waschini offspring. I have nothing to lose.

☾

Acaraho and Adia reached her quarters. It was late, and she was exhausted. Once she was safely in, she heard him exchange words with the guard who stood just outside. Usually, Acaraho retired to his quarters, taking his rest when she was taking hers. But for some reason, he relieved the standing guard of the evening shift and stationed himself at the entrance.

Adia dragged herself down the passage, eyes

downcast. The show of strength she had put on in the gathering room before leaving—her statement to Khon'Tor that if he did not honor his end of the bargain, she was released from hers—had been a last-ditch attempt to cover her concern at what she had just done. She was worried, but she did not want Khon'Tor to know that.

Nadiwani had been waiting for Adia's return.

"What's wrong? Did you ask Khon'Tor about the Whitespeak lessons for Oh'Dar? What happened?"

"Oh'Dar will get the Whitespeak training if Khon'Tor can find a teacher. I made that stipulation," said Adia.

It was late. "Is Oh'Dar still awake?" she asked Nadiwani. She wanted to cuddle him, hold him close.

"No, I'm sorry. He's fast asleep. But I can wake him if you want?"

"No. It's alright. I'm going to go to bed. Will you be staying up long?" Adia asked.

Nadiwani answered that she would be turning in shortly herself, so Adia lay down and prayed that sleep would come quickly.

☾

Whatever was going on, Adia was not talking about it. They usually shared everything, so this was a disturbing turn.

Adia had used the term stipulation. *Stipulation to what?* thought Nadiwani. Adia's use of the term made the Helper think of an agreement. *Has she had to make some kind of deal with Khon'Tor to gain his permission for Oh'Dar to learn Whitespeak?*

The minute she thought it, Nadiwani knew the answer. *Of course. Khon'Tor does not do anything for anyone without getting something in return*, she said to herself.

❂

Acaraho, Adia, Nadiwani, and Hakani all spent sleepless nights. Khon'Tor, on the other hand, slept like a rock.

❂

The next morning the community was still electrified with talk over what had taken place the night before. If Adia and Khon'Tor were prohibited from talking about what happened, all the others made up for the silence by talking about nothing else.

Those who witnessed it were full of conjecture over what this Rah-hora involved. All knew the rules of the Rah-hora. None of them had ever witnessed one being executed, and neither had the parents or grandparents of most. This was a rare event that would be talked about for generations to come.

Realizing Adia was not willing to talk about the night before, Nadiwani arose and sent word for one of the females to take over the care of Oh'Dar. If she could not find out here what had happened, she would go elsewhere. Someone had to know something.

She entered the Great Chamber, which was a roiling sea of clamor about what had occurred the previous night. She sat at one of the tables with the other females, piecing together what they said had happened between Khon'Tor and Adia. She learned that Adia had initiated a conversation and then Khon'Tor had initiated the Rah-hora. But even without knowing the details, Nadiwani still knew more than most. She knew Adia had been going to approach Khon'Tor about training for Oh'Dar. She knew from her conversation with Adia the night before that Khon'Tor had agreed to provide the training. What was missing was everything else in between. Rah-hora was only invoked when high-level agreements were made, or when one of the parties wanted to ensure there was no way for the other party to back out.

Since Khon'Tor initiated the Rah-hora, whatever Adia had to put up for her side of the bargain is something Khon'Tor wants very much. And whatever it was, at some point it is going to cost her greatly.

"Oh, Adia. What have you done?"

CHAPTER 12

Awaking at first light, Adia busied herself in her quarters, putting together the last items to go into the exchange basket in return for the warm weather wrappings Is'Taqa would soon bring. The weather had turned cold in the past few weeks, and she worried about Oh'Dar catching a chill. Even though the underground living area was a fairly constant temperature, it was on the cool side for the Brothers, which meant it would also be for Oh'Dar. In addition, cold breezes occasionally blew in, dropping the temperature several degrees. She wished she had thought to ask for furs and blankets. Perhaps she would ask Is'Taqa about this when she saw him.

Adia thought it odd that someone of the rank of Second Chief would be bringing her the wrappings. But then she realized he was one of only three

Brothers who knew a Waschini offspring was at Kthama.

Rising and seeing Nadiwani was gone, but that Haiwee was there to look after Oh'Dar, Adia decided to make her way to the Great Chamber. She needed to rest, but for some reason, she felt she had to get away. As she left, she was startled to see Acaraho, having forgotten he had relieved the previous night's guard.

For the second time in so few days, Acaraho and Adia made eye contact. As he looked into her eyes, she could not contain her feelings, and the tears welled up and spilled over. She was exhausted mentally, emotionally, and physically. Her reserves were gone, and her emotions were too close to the surface to veil.

Acaraho forgot himself and reached out to comfort her. He caught himself but not before his movement betrayed his intention.

Realizing he had been about to pull her into his arms, Adia so wished he had not stopped. She longed for even a moment's rest in the arms of this riveting man, whose presence was the only thing that made her feel safe anymore.

His expression of tenderness toward her broke her last shard of reserve. Adia turned and ran unceremoniously down the tunnel hallway.

She ducked into one of the small alcoves along the tunnel to pull herself together. She had to get herself back under control. Whatever other trials were ahead of her, it was a long way from over. She was so tired. And she was not feeling well: her head was spinning, and she felt hot, then cold. She just wanted to rest.

○

Back in the Great Chamber, one of the watchers was looking for Khon'Tor. Informed that the Leader was in his quarters, the watcher set out to find him. Everyone watching knew something else important must be afoot. Nobody hunted down Khon'Tor, Leader of the People of the High Rocks, in his private living spaces after-hours unless it was terribly important.

As the watcher approached Khon'Tor's quarters, he made a point of doing so noisily. He did not want to interrupt anything important that might be going on inside. Khon'Tor heard the male approaching and went into the hall to meet him, fully expecting it to be Acaraho, who should himself have risen by now.

Even before the watcher said a word, the alarm on his face and the fact that he was there told Khon'Tor something serious had happened.

"What is it, Akule?" asked Khon'Tor, hoping he had gotten the name right. He was not as close to Acaharo's guards and watchers as was the High Protector.

"Tell me what you need to, and quickly."

"I have a message from the High Council. I was told to come and tell you directly, no matter what. A contingent of Waschini has entered our territory," Akule explained. "They said it is the largest group they have ever seen until now. They are riding in on horseback. From the direction they were traveling, their route would bring them across our territory within a matter of a day or two."

"Thank you, Akule. Please go immediately to the High Chief Ogima Adoeete and make sure he also knows this. If Ogima Adoeete is not available for you to speak with directly, deliver the message either to their Second, Is'Taqa, or to their Medicine Woman."

Akule left to do as Khon'Tor had ordered. In earlier times—better times—Khon'Tor would have assembled the Healer and his mate Hakani as being Second and Third Rank. But as things were now, the only counsel Khon'Tor was interested in or had any faith in was Acaraho's. Knowing Acaraho would be in place guarding the Healer's Quarters, he sent a guard to relieve him.

Khon'Tor told Acaraho what Akule had relayed from the High Council. Acaraho listened and then spoke, "If the Waschini are riding that hard, they are most likely on their way somewhere specific and therefore just passing through."

Acaraho and Khon'Tor agreed it would be wise to bring everyone but the watchers inside and to forbid anyone to leave Kthama until they knew the Waschini riding party had left the territory.

Within moments, word had spread that Khon'Tor was calling yet another general assembly. Because it came on the heels of the previous night's event, everyone was convinced it had something to do with the drama that had happened between their Healer and their Leader.

Everyone was in place well before the assembly horn blew, and both Khon'Tor and Acaraho took the stage, standing side by side. Adia could not keep her eyes off the High Protector. From where she was standing, she had full view of both males, and it was impossible not to make a comparison. She noticed their similarities: how exceptionally tall they both were, with their broad, well-developed shoulders and chiseled physiques. Both were males of power and authority, and in size and strength they were almost interchangeable, but their hearts could not have been more different.

Khon'Tor raised his left arm in his usual signal for silence, and immediately the room hushed. Acaraho stood next to him, staring straight into the crowd.

Khon'Tor began. "Not long ago, I stood before you with Ogima Adoeete, High Chief of the Brothers, and brought you news from the High Council about the threat presented to our people by the Waschini. At that time, I also shared what we know of the Waschini—their cruelty, their savagery, their disregard for the rights of the lives of others. Though the Ancients did not know of the Whites, their having not yet come to our shores, they did know hard times would come to the People through some threat."

No one was looking around; they were all hanging onto Khon'Tor's every word. Many were trying to understand how what he was saying could be connected to the events of the night before.

"The watcher, Akule, brought word from the High Council that a Waschini riding party of some size has entered the outer edges of our territory. We believe they are only crossing our land as a means to their intended destination—though we have no way of knowing where or how far that lies," he continued.

"As a precaution, we are bringing everybody inside except the watchers. I am ordering each of you to stay in Kthama. We have every confidence that the Waschini will pass through without incident.

"We are not and have never been a people of aggression like the Waschini, and we will not engage them. We will not harm them. We will allow them to go on their way, and I will let you know when the threat has passed. To make sure there is no misunderstanding, anyone leaving Kthama without my direct permission, or the permission of Acaraho, will suffer *serious* consequences for their actions."

When Khon'Tor finished speaking, Acaraho

stepped forward. Adia noticed he did not have to raise his hand to command the attention of the People.

"Anyone and everyone currently outside, other than the watchers, is being located and brought inside as I speak. This is a time for all of us to come together in support of each other and in support of Khon'Tor," Acaraho announced.

After a couple of seconds pause, he added, "All my males in attendance here, report to my meeting room now. Thank you."

Before he stepped down, Acaraho lowered his eyes to break eye contact with the crowd, the signal he was done speaking, and then after a few seconds looked up and directly in Adia's direction.

On his way out, the guards started gathering around him. Acaraho surveyed them, then stopped and pulled aside First Guard Awan. Pointing in Adia's direction, he was obviously assigning Awan to her protection in his place. Adia realized that under these circumstances, Acaraho would be needed in his position as the High Protector. It was not lost on her that even with everything going on, he had not forgotten his commitment to protect her.

Adia wanted to get to her quarters quickly to let Nadiwani know what was going on, and she turned to leave, only to see Nadiwani and Khon'Tor's mate, Hakani, standing at the back of the room.

Where is Oh'Dar? Then Adia saw he was in the sling on Nadiwani's hip. *She had no one to leave him with since everyone was ordered to attend. All the offspring are here, but thank goodness he is being quiet.* The tide of favor had been turning in Oh'Dar's direction, and *this* was not the time for everyone to be reminded there was a Waschini in their midst.

The crowd remained for quite some time, discussing Khon'Tor's announcement.

One by one anyone outside was rounded up and brought inside by Acaraho's team.

Still early in the day, but tired from her lack of sleep the past night, Adia returned to her quarters to lie down to rest. She lay there replaying the events of the past few days.

Do the Waschini really pose a threat? Or are they riding through as everyone thinks? I know what they are capable of. I will never forget the sight of Oh'Dar's massacred parents. Slaughtered, butchered, left as carrion for the predators. But, Oh'Dar, there is no part of those monsters in you. I know it.

Just as she was about to fall asleep, Adia remembered the bag she had found among Oh'Dar's covers, the one which held the hard, oval-shaped item with the likenesses of Oh'Dar's parents in it. She had forgotten about it all this time, forgotten how she had stopped to bury it at the Healer's Cove, not daring to bring it to Kthama. *Oh no. What if the Waschini discover it? It could lead them here. They could find Kthama. They could take him from me!*

Adia had pushed herself so hard since rescuing Oh'Dar. She was determined to prove Khon'Tor wrong—that she could fully shoulder her responsibilities as Helper, as well as handling the primary responsibility for Oh'Dar. Already past her physical limits, the last few weeks had brought her to emotional and psychological exhaustion. Adia was convinced that if she did not go and retrieve the little bag and its contents, some great tragedy would ensue.

Even though she was not reasoning properly, she was still thinking— *I have to go and get the little pouch. But what about First Guard Awan? How am I going to get away from him?* She knew Acaraho had picked him as one who, if need be, would put his life on the line to protect her. Awan would not miss her leaving and would certainly not fall asleep at his post.

Adia had some time, knowing that her plan was best executed after nightfall when the darkness would be a disadvantage to the Waschini.

As she lay quietly putting together her plan of escape, Hakani was putting together a plan of her own.

🜚

She had stood in the back of the room listening to Khon'Tor address the People. Khon'Tor had stripped her of her position as Third Rank, and she was no longer recognized by him, or anyone else. She was effectively invisible. She had lost favor with the People through her actions with the Waschini offspring, though she blamed Adia and Khon'Tor for that outcome, not herself. Everyone knew Khon'Tor had expelled her from his bed. She was humiliated. Everything had turned against her.

In contrast, everything seemed to be going Khon'-Tor's way. Whatever the Rah-hora between him and the Healer, Khon'Tor had come out on top. His announcement of the Waschini threat validated everything he had warned them about since returning from the High Council meeting. He had spoken well and authoritatively. He had once again established himself as a great Leader in the eyes of the People.

While everything was turning in his favor, she was losing more and more ground. *Something must happen to bring Khon'Tor down. I cannot stand seeing him parade around like the glorious Leader. If only he would do something wrong. Something terribly, terribly wrong. Something so over the line that the People would never be able to overlook it—not even for the great Khon'Tor.*

Hakani knew that though he was riding high at the moment, it had been a long hard road of highs and lows over the past few seasons. She could see he was physically exhausted. He had to be close to his mental breaking point.

Everyone had a limit—even the strongest of the strong. If Hakani could only push him past his limit — No matter what she might have done wrong, she was still a female. And females were revered among the People. The People's laws and customs were established to honor and protect them. There were severe penalties for any male, no matter his station, who would strike a female.

Hakani knew she was walking a very dangerous line because Khon'Tor was a male of incredible strength. She was no match for him in any regard. If she drove him too far, too far into a rage, there was a risk she might pay for it with her life.

I have to chance it. Now is my opportunity to turn the tide against him. I might not get another one. He is at breaking point, I am sure of it. There might never be another period with so many challenges strung one after the other.

She had only one card left to use against him, and she had to make it count for all it was worth. She was ready. She was prepared to risk everything. All she needed now was for him to come back to their quarters.

And to hope she was as clever as she thought she was.

In the meantime, Adia had figured out her plan. Though she could not elude the guard, she might be able to trick him long enough to make her escape.

Nadiwani had come back to their quarters, but thinking Adia was finally sleeping she took Oh'Dar and left to visit Haiwee, giving Adia peace and quiet, hopefully to get the rest she so urgently needed.

Adia opened her eyes. She could tell that twilight was closing in by the quality of the light over the workspace. Though strangely unsteady on her feet, she hurried around her quarters, gathering up the items she needed and then scurried through the door to where Awan was standing.

As she stepped out in front of him, the First Guard brought himself back to full attention, looking straight over her head as was the custom. Knowing he would follow her, Adia walked down the tunnel from her quarters toward the main assembly area, the Great Chamber. But just before reaching the main room, still carrying the bundle she had brought with her, she took a turn down a different tunnel.

The guard stopped dead in his tracks.

Adia smiled. She knew exactly what the problem was. She had entered the tunnel to the females' bathing area. It was forbidden to males, without exception. The guard could not go with her.

Adia looked up at him and blinked. "It's alright, I understand. You may wait here."

So he took his position there and waited, knowing there was no other exit.

Except that he was wrong.

❂

No one knew the tunnels as well as the Healer did. Not every twist and turn. And when it came to the females' personal areas, the males barely knew them at all. Some of the other females might know what she did about this particular area—if they ever thought about it—but they were not there.

Adia padded down the tunnel into the bathing area. She looked longingly at the clear, cool water, wishing she had time to stop and bathe. She was perspiring and felt overheated. Her body was starting to ache.

The Mother Stream was the lifeblood of the People's existence, bringing in as it did plenty of oxygen and fresh water. This private bathing area that Adia now entered was one of the modifications made by the People over time.

Inflowing water has to flow out or become stagnant, and Adia knew there was an exit through the channel which returned the stream to the outside. She also knew that because the opening had been manually constructed, it was large enough for someone to travel along without having to get into the water. Once outside, the stream had been diverted away and there was a little private alcove, protected from the watchers' eyes by an upper outcropping of rock. The females used this area to dry more quickly in the summer heat without fear of being seen.

The People were not particularly fond of swimming. They were too muscular and had little buoyancy. But they did enjoy a soothing, cooling soak, and it was for this purpose the bathing areas had been built—one for the females and one for the males.

Adia set down the items she had brought with her. They were mostly meant as a distraction though, and because when she came back in, she wanted something larger in which to conceal the little bag with the oval picture frames. She planned to return through the same channel. Since there was ample walking area on each side, coming back against the direction of the water would not be a problem. She would not even have to get wet if she was careful.

Though she was exhausted, distraught, and now becoming physically sick, her mind had been working clearly enough to design and execute this plan.

I must hurry. I cannot be gone too long. I do not know when Awan might decide I am taking too long and find someone to send in and check on me.

The Healer picked her way down the side of the circulation channel and came out exactly where she had thought she would. She breathed a sigh of relief and started making her way to the Healers Cove.

Her plan was working perfectly.

Until Akule, returning from delivering the

message of the Waschini riding party to the Brothers' High Chief, saw her outside Kthama.

○

While Adia was congratulating herself on eluding her guard, Hakani was waiting for Khon'Tor to return to their shared quarters. She was counting on his exhaustion to drive him back there, despite their estranged relationship. He would need sleep, and the little bit of comfort provided by his own bed would hopefully prove irresistible.

○

Just before twilight, Khon'Tor did return to their room. He had spent the remainder of the day with Acaraho, and all the People had been accounted for. Only the guards were still outside, and Akule had not yet returned with word that High Chief Ogima Adoeete now knew of the Waschini riding party. Acaraho had arranged for scheduled updates, and now Khon'Tor was indeed exhausted.

He wanted only one thing—to sleep and not think another thought. Grateful that Acaraho was in charge of organizing everything, Khon'Tor was beyond doing much of anything right now, but certainly did not want anyone to know.

Though he had enjoyed irritating Hakani the night before, he was too tired to take up the sport again tonight. He hoped she would not be there when he returned, and he was disappointed to find she was. He decided he would try not to rile her, in hopes that he could get his much-needed rest.

○

Hakani could hardly contain her excitement that Khon'Tor had returned to their quarters. Her heart was starting to beat quickly. She knew she had to be very careful with her next moves so as not to trigger any suspicions that she was up to something.

She waited until he had finished his preparation for sleep; she did not want any distractions once she had put her plan in motion.

Sitting up on her sleeping mat, Hakani startled Khon'Tor by speaking. "Your speech tonight was impressive," she said, though the word she used was a combination of the meaning of impressive, reassuring, and commanding as if befitting a strong Leader.

He did not acknowledge her remark. *Last night she hated me, tonight she is praising me?*

"I found myself wishing I was standing by your side again," she added.

Khon'Tor snorted. *I am too tired to try to keep up with this female's changing moods. The last time she was nice to me, she created that debacle with the Waschini offspring. And our relationship has been in a downward spiral ever since,* he thought to himself.

"I am exhausted, Hakani. I am turning in."

He then lay down in his sleeping area, hoping Hakani would either leave their quarters entirely or at least lie back down in her area and leave him alone. It was unusual for him to retire this early, but he was drained and knew trying days were still ahead.

He stretched out, enjoying the welcoming pleasure of the soft bed. Other than mealtimes, it was his only physical comfort. He breathed in deeply, inhaling its pleasant, natural fragrance. He knew he would be asleep in moments.

Khon'Tor awoke to the warmth of a body pressed up against the full length of his back. It took him a moment to surface. Then he realized some female was in bed with him—Hakani. She had come to his sleeping area and was nestled up against him, her arm across his in a position of embrace. He shook his head to clear the cobwebs. *Am I dreaming this? What is going on?*

Khon'Tor realized Hakani had intentionally woken him. She had slipped her arm across his shoulder and curled her fingers through the hair on his chest. She pressed herself up harder against him, an old signal between them that she wanted him.

There is no mistaking what she is doing. She has finally come to my bed. She has finally surrendered and is offering herself to me! He was almost too exhausted to respond, but the years of her denying him won out.

Khon'Tor rolled over to face Hakani and meet her embrace. No matter how much he still hated her, he needed this more. All the suppressed tension welled up in him, and he was immediately ready and fully enabled to complete the bond. If he had not been so exhausted, he would have had his guard up —but he was too far past reasonable thought. He was responding to a primal need—one that had gone unsatisfied for far too long.

As he rolled over to face her, she moved into a position that made herself fully available to him. Khon'Tor shifted his large frame over hers, completely covering Hakani's body with his. He pressed himself against her. He was one motion away from mating her. His pulse was racing; he was breathing deeply and quickly in anticipation. In one movement it would be done, and then after all the frustration, built up over years of her denial, he would find some release. *Finally*.

As Khon'Tor moved over her, Hakani raised her head against his neck, as if to meet his embrace. Her warm breath in his ear increased the pressure about to explode from inside him.

Just as he was about to take her, he heard her whisper, "No, Khon'Tor. No. Stop. I've changed my mind. I do not give my consent."

Khon'Tor froze. His blood ran cold.

It took every bit of will to stop his forward motion. He held himself completely still. Surely he could not have heard her correctly. *How could this be? There is no way I misinterpreted her actions—she wanted me; everything she did signaled her consent. She came to me! How can she now be saying no?*

Khon'Tor quickly pulled himself away from her, putting enough distance between them to ensure there was no way his body could overrule his will and complete the act.

The female had said *no*. If he continued, he would be breaking the Sacred Law of the People: Never Without Consent. His mind and his pulse now racing equally, he pushed himself up on one arm to face her directly.

"What did you say?" he demanded, but he knew full well what she had said. He knew he had not misunderstood her, but he needed to hear it from her clearly, in full voice, not delivered as a whisper in the dark between past lovers.

"I said no, Khon'Tor. I have changed my mind. I withdraw my consent. I do not wish to mate with you," she stated.

Khon'Tor was a hair's breadth away from breaking point. He looked at her squarely. He could see clearly that she was smiling smugly at him, a look of twisted satisfaction on her face.

It now dawned on him. Hakani had never intended to mate with him. She had meant to lead him on to believe she would, only to stop him, to deliver her denial at the final, most vulnerable of moments.

She had almost won, had he not been able to stop himself, he would have broken First Law. He would be utterly dishonored, even more so for the position of authority he held.

So this had been her cruel game. Had she waited a moment longer, in another movement, I would have completed the act. But Hakani spoke too soon. I did not mate her after she withdrew her consent.

Khon'Tor, as angry as he was, breathed a huge sigh of relief. He had almost made the biggest mistake of his life, orchestrated by this female lying next to him. But it had not worked, and she had not won. He had prevailed despite all her clever tricks and scheming.

There were no words to express his hatred of her now. He was furious at her charade, at being set up by her, at the pleasure he knew she took both in planning and in executing her clever act. He was angry with himself for dropping his guard and believing anything with her was as it appeared. He had been played for a fool; he should know better by now. Hakani was consumed by her intention to destroy him. She hated him and would hate him until she took her last breath. Maybe even beyond. But this last plan of hers settled it in his mind. There would never be peace between them. *It is just a matter of time before she tries something else.*

After the stunt she pulled with the Waschini offspring, he had stripped his need for her down to one thing—her ability to provide him with a male offspring. This last trick fully demonstrated that she would never willingly fulfill that role for him. *She has no further purpose in my life. Continuing to share quarters with her will only give her the opportunity of more attempts to destroy me. Eventually, she will find a way to succeed.*

Khon'Tor sighed. *It is time to approach the High Council and request Bak'tah-Awhidi. But I will set her up in her own quarters—and continue to provide for her maintenance and basic needs—with or without the High Council's consent. Otherwise, I am done with her.*

He rose from the bed and turned to look down at his mate, making it a point to tower intimidatingly over her. "Your trick did not work Hakani; I honored your refusal, and I have committed no crime," he stated. Though his voice was controlled, it still betrayed the anger of which he was barely in control.

Hakani did not say a word, just smiled smugly at him.

"Are you so sure, Khon'Tor?" she asked, mocking him.

"I am very sure," he replied. "You should have waited longer. You could have dragged this on for years yet, but now you have tipped your hand. You have made my path very clear. You will never give me offspring, and that was the last use I had for you," he continued. "I told you I would have no qualms going to the High Council, setting you aside as First Choice and taking a second mate," he said harshly. "They will grant Bak'tah-Awhidi on the basis that you are barren, considering that you have not so far produced an heir."

"Oh, and how will you win your case when I am standing next to you, clearly carrying your offspring?"

Khon'Tor knew she was bluffing. He had stopped himself. There was no way she could be with offspring. It had been ages.

"Well," she added, "At least they will *assume* this is your offspring. And only you and I will know it is not."

Khon'Tor's eyes darkened with rage, his muscles tensed, adrenaline flooded his brain. His hatred reached boiling point and flashed over. *She betrayed me by lying with another male—and now I will have to accept another man's offspring as my own?*

He no longer cared about consequences; at that moment he only wanted to crush her neck with his bare hands, eviscerate her head to toe with his teeth, and watch her lifeblood leak out across the floor— taking to *krell* with her whatever bastard offspring she carried.

🌀

There was little doubt that had someone not pounded furiously on the door of their quarters, in another few seconds Hakani would have lain dying, drowning in a pool of her own blood.

No one ever pounded on the door of the Leader's private quarters. Such an unprecedented action could only be warranted by an emergency of epic proportions.

The shock of such a breach in protocol startled Khon'Tor just long enough for a crack of control to reestablish itself in his brain. Tearing his attention away from Hakani, who still lay on his bed, braced for his assault on her, he launched himself at the stone slab door and flung it open.

For the second time that day, Akule had violated the privacy of Khon'Tor's living quarters.

The watcher stood there petrified, eyes open as far as they would go, staring up at the angriest male he had ever seen in his life. Akule at first mistook Khon'-Tor's intense rage as directed at him for his intrusion into the Leader's private quarters. But then his eyes glanced past Khon'Tor and noticed Hakani lying on the bed. Seeing her there, coupled with Khon'Tor's highly impassioned state, he misinterpreted for a second time the reason for Khon'Tor's rage.

"My deepest apologies, Adoeete," he stammered, stepping back into the hallway in an attempt to put some distance between himself and this hulking, enraged man.

Khon'Tor followed him into the hallway, quickly pulling the stone door back in place behind him, cutting off Akule's view of Hakani.

"Adoeete, I have delivered the message about the Waschini riding party to the Brothers—"

"*That* is what you came here to tell me?" Khon'Tor practically roared the question at Akule. Then he braced his arm against the wall and leaned his head against it.

"No, Adoeete. But I thought you might want to know. What I really came here to tell you is that I just saw the Healer leaving Kthama."

Khon'Tor heard the words Akule was speaking but could not quite believe them. *Against his strictest orders, Adia had left Kthama.*

He was still fighting for control; still desperately wanting to return inside and crush the life out of Hakani. But some presence of mind was creeping back. He found out from Akule where he had seen Adia and the direction in which she was headed. Then he commanded the watcher to tell no one of this.

"No one else must know this, not even Acaraho," Khon'Tor said. "Go and relieve the guard at the front entrance and send him to his quarters," he added.

Whatever he was going to do about Adia, he knew he must be able to do it without any further complications. So he set off alone to find her and bring her back.

Akule walked away, feeling lucky to be alive and thinking how wrong the rumors were regarding the state of the Leader's relationship with his mate Hakani. From what he had seen of Khon'Tor's impassioned state just then, the Leader and his mate were anything but estranged!

Akule was three for three in his misinterpretations of what had been going on in the Leader's private quarters that evening.

Adia picked her way carefully along the treacherous, snow-covered path. The cold weather and her weakened condition slowed her travel considerably. The snow that had begun falling earlier in the day had left a slippery coating everywhere.

Once at the Healer's cove, she hurried to where she had buried the little bag. She pawed through the soil and pulled it out. Though no one else but Nadiwani ever came to this place, Adia carefully patted the soil back, so it did not appear disturbed. Clutching the pouch, she left the Healer's Cove and set off on her way back to Kthama, remembering she needed to return through the tunnel exiting from the females' bathing pool.

Luckily, considering her weakening state, she

only had to retrace the tracks she had left in the snow on her way there.

The same tracks Khon'Tor had no trouble following either—tracks that led him directly to her.

Khon'Tor planted himself a few feet ahead of her, snow falling gently around him, waiting for her to look up and see him. He stood with feet apart, arms crossed in front of his chest; an angry, immovable object completely blocking her way.

Walking with her head down to make sure she did not lose her footing on the slippery path, Adia ran smack into Khon'Tor, almost knocking herself off balance. Her head shot up, and she looked directly into the hard, bitter eyes of the towering Khon'Tor.

She tried to back away, but he quickly grabbed her wrists in an iron grip and jerked her to him, effectively holding her captive. Her eyes widened. Noticing she was holding something, he transferred her wrists to one hand, and forcing her palm open with the other, he exposed the pouch that contained the locket.

"What is this?" he demanded, jerking it out of her hand.

He continued to hold her wrists tightly together as he angrily ripped the leather pouch open with his teeth, a shiny object falling to the ground. He bent over to pick up what was left of the pouch and tossed it angrily as hard as he could out into the treetops below the path. Still holding Adia, he retrieved the locket, lifting it to his eyes. It twisted on the end of its chain. He could not tell what it was made of, but he knew it was Waschini. There was a likeness of a male and female drawn or carved into it. He could not tell the method, but he knew what he was looking at.

The Healer was headed back to Kthama, so he knew she must previously have left it somewhere and was returning after retrieving it. This must have something to do with the Waschini offspring, but he could not figure out why she would come out in this weather, directly defying him, to get it.

Adia struggled against Khon'Tor but could not free herself from his iron clasp. He knew he was hurting her, but he did not care.

"Why would you do this? As if it was not bad enough bringing that creature here. You also had to bring *this back with it*?" With the locket clutched in his fist, he shook it in front of her face.

"You are out of your mind! Whatever this is, it is a tie to his family. This can *identify* him," Khon'Tor continued.

He angrily released her wrists, giving her a backward thrust as he did, causing her to lose her balance and fall to the ground. He turned his back on her, fists now clutched against tightly closed eyes.

Everyone, even the most powerful and disciplined, even one possessing the strongest will, has a limit. The Alpha of the People of the High Rocks was no exception. And he had already been brought to the edge once earlier at the hands of Hakani. Had Akule not showed up when he did, in another second Khon'Tor would have collected the ultimate price from his mate for her betrayal.

Khon'Tor's emotions filled with every affront, insult, and challenge he had experienced at the hands of these two females.

The pain of his original desire for Adia, believing she would be his only to have her snatched away from him at the last minute—chosen to become the People's Healer, forever out of reach. Then having to pick another in her stead, hiding his disappointment and despair—a decision forced in haste and one that had paired him with a bitter, resentful female who hated him for reasons he could not understand.

His mind went back to when she had brought the offspring into their community, insolently breaking the laws and getting away with it—still managing to win the People's favor. Succeeding despite every hardship he put on her.

Hakani, creating a dramatic scene with the Waschini offspring in front of the entire community with no regard for the position into which it put him. His mate's denial of him year after year, and then finally tonight, knowing how exhausted he was and how much strain he was under, offering him release and leading him on only to refuse him at the last second. The assaults on his pride, his position, and his authority kept coming. Hakani betraying him by lying with another, and now taunting him with this other man's offspring—an offspring she would claim as his, and who would be heir to his leadership.

Years of battling these females, thinking he had first one then the other under control, only to have them defy him again and again.

The rage that had fueled his desire to kill Hakani, and which Akule had thwarted by pounding on the door of his quarters, had resurfaced with a vengeance. Rage that had never found its outlet; never found its release.

And now this. Disobeying a direct order given publicly in front of the full community. *His order! Again, defying him directly!*

All the frustration, challenge, and betrayal— regardless of at which female's hand—churned together into one seething mass and Khon'Tor was losing the ability to tell them apart. The two females who were the source of all his troubles and hard- ships, his anger, and his longing were becoming confused in his mind. The betrayal of him by one had become that of the other; swirling together, intermixing until he could no longer separate his anger with one from his anger with the other.

Khon'Tor turned back expecting to find Adia crumpled on the ground in the accumulating snow. Just as he turned, Adia had managed to raise herself up, and in trying to gain her balance, placed her hand directly on the center of his chest to steady herself. His last thread of control snapped at the contact of Adia's warm hand; his mind, relinquished its hold on reality, ceded to his overwhelming urges.

Her hand on his chest became Hakani's hand on his chest earlier—stirring him, inviting him, deceiving him into believing she wanted him, only to reject and humiliate him in the next moment.

Adia became Hakani and Hakani became Adia. Adia was teasing him, leading him on as Hakani had done.

Khon'Tor's anger exploded; he pushed Adia away roughly, bellowing, "No!" And he pulled his arm back and hit her across the side of her face, knocking her the rest of the way to the ground. Had she not already been falling as his hand made contact, no doubt his blow would have killed her right there.

Adia hit the ground hard.

She raised herself on one elbow and looked up at him through glazed eyes, blood streaming profusely from the side of her head and dripping onto the rocks beside her.

"Khon'Tor—" Her voice was barely audible.

Khon'Tor looked down at her, sprawled on the ground in front of him. Hurt, weak, defenseless; he should have felt sorry for her, but he felt nothing of the kind. The blood lust he felt for Hakani was surging again through every part of him. He had been pushed past the point of no return—past his breaking point.

Khon'Tor's mind finally snapped. While he had wanted to kill Hakani, tear her apart, slice her open top to bottom, her blood flowing everywhere, Khon'Tor did not want to kill Adia. His murderous rage had turned into something entirely different that he wanted to do to her.

The object of his desire, the female he could never have, his First Choice, lay helpless in front of him. And there was nothing and *no one*, not even himself, to stop him from taking what he wanted— what should have been his long ago.

Khon'Tor took domination of Adia, claiming by force the maiden after whom he had lusted for years. He turned his will to the satisfaction of his animal desires.

Adia had known she must get back to the safety of Kthama. *Khon'Tor will be so angry if he finds out I left against his orders.*

Then, just as she had been thinking about him, he was standing over her. *What is happening?*

Adia was already confused from the sickness that was taking hold, but the blow to her head put her into a dazed state of half twilight. As she was losing consciousness, she felt a tremendous weight move over her, so warm in the winter night, comforting at first, but then almost crushing her. And after that, pressure, unbelievable pressure, followed by a blindingly sharp pain she could never have imagined; pain that pierced her straight up through her center.

And then more pressure, splitting her in two. And again, hard, painful thrusts rocking her body against the cold, harsh ground.

Adia finally slipped into total darkness, just as Khon'Tor's massive body tightened, stiffened against her and then froze—suspended in a moment of complete, unequaled release as he spent all his anger and rage deep inside her—*Without Her Consent.*

CHAPTER 13

Is'Taqa was approaching Kthama with the wrappings for Oh'Dar when he noticed Khon'Tor walking away from Kthama. Puzzled by where the great Leader of the People would be going at this time, and wishing to greet him, Is'Taqa followed him down a long, seldom-used path.

Not being able to keep up with the bigger male, just as he was about to call out to Khon'Tor, he saw the Leader stop as another, smaller figure came up from the other direction and ran smack into him.

What Is'Taqa thought was almost comical quickly took a dark turn. He stood there horrified as he watched Khon'Tor overpower the smaller figure and roughly throw him to the hard ground. When the smaller male struggled back to his feet, Khon'Tor knocked him back to the ground again with one swift blow to the head.

Is'Taqa, not having the low light sight of the

People and with the snow falling heavily, could make out the gross motions of what was going on but not the details. But as he watched what Khon'Tor did next, Is'Taqa's blood ran cold. What he saw unfold was inconceivable—maybe not for the Waschini, but so far out of the People's realm of possibility.

He froze as he watched the abomination being carried out before him.

Is'Taqa did not want to believe what he was seeing, but there was no misinterpreting what was taking place. The positions of the two bodies, the movements, the final hold and telltale culminating release of the much larger figure left no doubt about the violation that was taking place.

This was not a fight between two males.

Violence against the females of the People was virtually unheard of and was a serious enough crime. *But this?* This was beyond the pale.

When he saw Khon'Tor turn back to come his way, Is'Taqa ducked behind a rocky outcropping at the side of the path.

○

Khon'Tor removed himself from Adia and stood up, for a moment looking down at her as she lay in front of him. His mind started to clear, now relieved of the blinding instincts that had overpowered it moments earlier.

The female was not moving. Though he did not

see how it was possible, he wondered if he might have killed her.

Even at the apex of his rage when his mind snapped, he had never wanted to kill Adia. Hakani yes, but Adia, no. Overpower Adia? Yes. Subjugate her? Yes. Defeat her? Yes. Demonstrate complete power over her, inflict his will over her, and violate her in the most intimate, humiliating way possible— yes, *yes*, *yIses*, to all of it.

But never to kill her.

Khon'Tor bent back down to examine her. She was still breathing. There was blood everywhere; all over the path, the rocks, the side of her face. And now that he was seeing her more clearly, he realized she was physically ill. He had never known Adia to be sick, but there was no doubt that she was at the moment definitely so, and perhaps seriously.

He ran his hand slowly up over his forehead and back through the silver hair that crowned his head.

When, in his enraged state, the two females had merged into one, Khon'Tor had not been able to separate his anger toward them. He recognized that the rage he had been denied inflicting on Hakani had combined with his anger at Adia and that he had spent it all on Adia instead.

Yes, Adia had defied him by leaving Kthama when he had made it clear that no one should. Yes, she had shown terrible judgment *once again,* this time by wanting to bring a Waschini item back with her that was connected directly to the offspring. One that could potentially lead the Waschini to him. It was a long shot, but it was possible. And as Leader, Khon'Tor always had to think in terms of possibilities——no matter how remote they might seem to someone not in his position.

He slumped over, holding his head in his hands. *I am tired of all the complications, tired of all the battles with moves and countermoves, always struggling to stay one step ahead of everyone else. Worrying about what these two females will do next. I just need it to end.*

He did not want to think any longer, least of all about Hakani waiting back in their quarters. Having to face her again, knowing she was carrying another man's offspring. Knowing she would claim it as heir to the leadership—his leadership. *Years and years ahead of me, living with that lie? Wondering, every time I look at her and the offspring, which of the males betrayed me.*

Khon'Tor scoffed. It was not her infidelity that hurt; he truly could not care less who she mated with. It was knowing that somewhere, out among all the males of the community—males whom he had hunted with, defended their females and offspring with, males whom he had trusted—one of them had committed the ultimate act of disloyalty by lying with his mate. Each time he looked into the eyes of any male, he would wonder, *Was it you? Were you the one*?

Khon'Tor forced his thoughts back to the moment at hand. What about her? What about Adia

—the female he had wanted all these years, now lying at his feet possibly dying by his acts.

He knew she had blacked out—but at what point? Was she aware that in her moment of total defenselessness, he had not helped her, but instead—

Khon'Tor's heart started pounding again as his mind raced. Instead of being remembered as the great Leader, his name would go down in history as breaking the most revered of the First Laws: Never Without Consent.

Oh but not just any female. This was Adia. One of the greatest of the People's Healers. A Healer, who was always chosen as a maiden and who was directed by law to remain so until her death. Beloved daughter of the great Apenimon'Mok, Leader of the People of the Deep Valley; a male whose legacy he struggled to live up to as it was.

He had defiled the great Leader's daughter— possibly even killed her.

And he, Khon'Tor, was not just any man. He was their Leader. He was in the highest position of authority. His People looked up to him to guide them, protect them. It was his responsibility to enforce the laws that had been established to protect their society and each of them individually—not to break the laws by committing an act of cowardice against someone who was utterly unable to defend herself. Even in the best state of health or presence of mind, any female of the People was no match for any of the males. And only a handful of the males of the community would have been able to defend themselves against Khon'Tor.

There would be no forgiveness for him. Not from the High Council, not from the females of the community, nor from the males. Not from anyone, ever.

Khon'Tor looked down at Adia, at the fallen snowflakes that clung to her everywhere. He wondered if she was dying.

All these thoughts and emotions and memories passed through Khon'Tor's mind in seconds. What felt like hours had taken up only a brief moment in time.

Then Khon'Tor's iron will and self-preservation kicked in—as it always did. After a few moments, his thoughts came back to his own problems and his own needs.

It would do no good to allow myself to be destroyed by this. Other than satisfying a need for justice, nothing good could come out of making known what I have done. It would certainly not help the People. If they have ever needed a strong Leader, with the threat of the Waschini at their door, now is the time. There is no one else who could take my place. Maybe Acaraho. He is as smart and as good a strategist as I am. He is a match physically, and he has the courage of the bravest warrior. He is respected and looked up to by everyone. But he is not of a Leader's bloodline. No. I am the only one who can lead them.

In a flash, all Khon'Tor's self-doubt disappeared.

No purpose will be served by allowing this to come to light. The loss of my leadership would cost the People more than the loss of the Healer.

Khon'Tor began immediately to consider his options. He thought and carefully thought over what had taken place.

No one other than Akule knows the Healer left the cave. No one other than Akule knows I went after her. There is no one else out here; Acaraho had everyone brought inside.

Khon'Tor then noticed the blood on the side of her head and the surrounding rocks. *Her wounds are consistent with having fallen and struck her head against one of those rocks. There are no other obvious injuries —and it would not occur to most to look for the unobvious one.*

He realized now that she had been sick when she left Kthama. There was a good chance someone else had noticed it and would remember.

But why did she leave Kthama; why is she out here alone and sick in this weather, and under the conditions of the lock-down I established. What was so important that she defied me again?

Khon'Tor remembered the locket. As much as he wanted to fling it into the valley below, he knew he had to leave it. It was the only explanation for her being out here.

The last he remembered was dangling it in front of her face just before he shoved her to the ground in anger.

He stooped down, his hands sweeping the ground. His fingers touched the cold, hard metal. He took the locket and curled it into the palm of her outstretched hand, ensuring it would not go unnoticed.

Then he stepped back and looked down at the scene. *It will be hours before anyone else comes this way. By then, with her already being sick, the blow to her head, all that blood, and the cold, all they will find will be her dead body and the Waschini locket in her palm.*

Satisfied there was nothing else to do, Khon'Tor took one last look at Adia and walked away, leaving her to die.

Is'Taqa was well hidden as Khon'Tor walked right by him.

After the Leader had passed and was far out of sight, Is'Taqa went to the prone figure and saw it was Adia.

When Khon'Tor had arranged the locket in her hand, though he could not see what it was, Is'Taqa had realized the Leader was staging a scene. Now considering the area of the blow to her head, and that she had fallen conveniently close to a grouping of rocks and bled all over them, the most obvious thing was to make it look like an accident. That she had fallen, been knocked unconscious, and died of exposure. It might just work for Khon'Tor. And the longer it took for someone to find her, the more sense it would make. Had Is'Taqa not seen and followed Khon'Tor here, there would be no one to challenge the story this setting was arranged to tell.

Is'Taqa checked her pulse. He placed the back of his hand against the cheek which had not been bloodied. *Cool to the touch but not yet cold.* He did not have the strength to carry her. All he could do was hurry to the People's cave without catching up to Khon'Tor and act as if he had come across her by accident on his way there.

He went back to the bundle of wrappings. He had brought three wolf pelts as a surprise. He picked the largest two and covered Adia up as best he could to maintain as much of her core temperature as possible. His heart was beating hard enough that he feared it would explode, but he had to give Khon'Tor time to get back first. And he had to be careful to support the story Khon'Tor had created, that she had been hurt in an accident.

Finally, calculating how long it had been and considering the length of Khon'Tor's stride, he figured enough time had passed, and he made his way to get help.

Akule was the only person who could reveal that Khon'Tor knew Adia had left and that the Leader had gone to look for her. On his way back, Khon'Tor grappled with what to do about him. Somehow he had to ensure the watcher's allegiance. There were only two ways Khon'Tor knew to do that—either offering something of value Akule could not refuse or by threatening him somehow. By the time Kthama's entrance was before him, Khon'Tor had still not decided which tack he would take.

As ordered, Akule had relieved the earlier guard. This had been an incredibly long day for the watcher, filled with one stressful moment after the next. When Khon'Tor finally arrived, Akule wanted to ask if he had found Adia, but it was not his place to do so.

"I could not find her," Khon'Tor volunteered. "It is too dangerous out there now. The snow has made everything slippery and treacherous. I will send a complement out in the morning. There is nothing else I can do," he added, carefully watching for Akule's reaction as he spoke. Trying to determine if the watcher could tell he was lying.

Out of nowhere, unbidden, Acaraho came running toward the two males. He was visibly alarmed and making a beeline for Khon'Tor.

Too much time had passed; Adia's guard, Awan, who was waiting for her to reappear from the females' bathing area, had become worried. He summoned one of the passing females to go and check, but she came back out stating there was no one there—only a pile of wrappings that had been left on the ledge.

"Adia is gone," shouted Acaraho across the distance, not waiting to reach Khon'Tor and Akule.

Almost at the same time, Is'Taqa rushed in, out of breath.

Khon'Tor froze, bearing down within himself, willing himself not to speak. Anything he said might give something away. He had learned that in times like this, it was best to hear what everyone else had to say and then to contribute as little as possible.

"Khon'Tor!" panted Is'Taqa, addressing him first as the highest-ranking person inside the Great Entrance. "Please come quickly. The Healer has fallen and hit her head. She is very ill; there is little time."

"Guards!" Acaraho bellowed across the hall, shattering the silence with the booming command. Within seconds, guards came out of nowhere, storming in his direction.

"You, you, you," pointing at three of them, "Remain here at the entrance. *No one* leaves, understood?"

"You," pointing to a fourth, "Go and find Nadiwani. Take one of the females with you to care for the offspring and let Nadiwani know Adia has been injured and to prepare for her care."

"You," he said, pointing to yet another. "You come with me. Is'Taqa, lead the way; let's go!" and with that, the four males were out of the entrance on their way to where Adia lay dying.

Acaraho was praying harder than he ever had in his life that she would be found alive—that he would get to her in time to save her. And as hard as Acaraho was praying that she would be found alive, Khon'Tor was praying she would not.

In that short time, the snow had started falling more heavily. Not able to keep up with the larger People, Is'Taqa explained to Acaraho where Adia was and caught up with them as soon as he could. Had it not been for Is'Taqa, it might have been some time before she was found as the snowfall had completely covered all the earlier tracks.

Despite his haste to access the extent of Adia's injuries, Acaraho took a few precious seconds to pass his eyes over her and the scene surrounding her, long enough to burn a picture of it into his memory before anything was touched. His eyes immediately spotted the shiny locket that lay curled up in her open palm.

He memorized every detail. How she was lying, the location and distance of the rocks, the amount of blood on her as opposed to the amount covering her surroundings, the way her head was turned, the direction her feet were pointing—every detail. In the few seconds he took to do this, he absorbed not only the location and depth of the blow to her head but also every visible scratch and wound on her, looking for any evidence that a physical assault had taken place. Evidence of assault—except the one assault it would never occur to most males to look for.

Acaraho then checked Adia's pulse, releasing a sigh of relief. He took the locket out of her hand and gave it to Is'Taqa. Then he lifted her carefully, along with the fur wraps with which Is'Taqa had covered her, and carried her back to Kthama in his arms, carefully picking his way along the slippery path.

Everything screamed to him that this was not an accident. Yes, it had been staged to look like one. And it was possible Adia had fallen and hit her head at some point—but there was more to it than that. She had been lying on her back, and the wound on the side of her head could not be missed—someone had arranged her like that. The locket neatly curled up in her open palm also seemed too obvious. Acaraho knew there was a story there *someone* did not want told. Someone was responsible for at least some part of her injury and did not want it known.

Nadiwani was as ready as she could be by the time they brought Adia to her. It took only seconds to see that the Healer was in grave danger. She had lost a fair amount of blood from the wound to her head, and she had lost too much body heat. But there was something else at play aside from her head wound and being chilled—she was also deathly ill from something in general.

Is'Taqa, Acaraho, and Khon'Tor were standing around anxiously waiting for Nadiwani to tell what she could see about Adia's condition—though each was on edge for different reasons.

Is'Taqa was one of three people in the room who knew what had really happened—Adia, who was unable to respond right now, himself, and Khon'Tor. If Adia never recovered, if the worst happened, that left only Is'Taqa to reveal the truth.

Acaraho had taken a position over against the wall where he usually stood when in the Healer's Quarters. He did not want to be in the way, but he was also struggling to maintain his composure and did not want the others to see.

Acaraho was filled with regret and self-blame even though he knew he'd had to take charge of the lock-down Khon'Tor had ordered. *If I had not turned Adia's protection over to someone else, she would never have left Kthama. She would not have been able to elude me. At the very least, if she had convinced me of the importance of that trinket she went to retrieve, I would have gone with her. And then whoever thought to attack her would have had to deal with me first.*

Now, because he had been pulled away from watching over her, Adia was perhaps dying in front of him. *Regardless of what happens, whether she lives or dies, I will find out who did this to her, and I will kill him myself. Slowly.*

Having finished her examination, Nadiwani turned to the others.

"Adia has lost a fair amount of blood. Her core temperature is low—too low. On top of that and her other obvious injuries, she is very sick. I imagine she was sick before she even left Kthama," she explained.

"I can treat the sickness and hope she has the strength to fight it off. But I need to get her core temperature up—and fast," she continued.

"How do you do that?" asked Is'Taqa. He was sibling to the Brothers' Medicine Woman, and he knew Ithua would heat stones in a fire and use them to warm the bed, but he also knew the People seldom used fire inside Kthama.

"The fastest way is with body heat," she said. "I need someone to lie with her and transfer his body heat to hers. The larger the body surface and the more muscular, the better," she added, looking directly over at Acaraho.

Is'Taqa was off the hook; needing body size and muscle mass she would never choose a Brother over one of the People.

However, the two largest most powerfully-built males in the community were standing right there in the room. Considering the tension between Khon'Tor and Adia, Nadiwani did not trust him for a second when it came to anything to do with Adia's welfare, nor could she expect him to suspend his duties as Leader of the People to stay there overnight. The obvious choice was Acaraho.

"Khon'Tor, Acaraho is already assigned to protecting Adia most of the time. And I cannot have just anyone in the Healer's Quarters. I also cannot have just any male do this—it has to be someone above reproach. There is no one more honorable than Acaraho."

The idea of a male lying in bed with a female with whom he was not paired was unthinkable, but this was a medical emergency. When it came to the Healer's practices, they were considered above reproach, and their orders were executed without question. Luckily, among the People, there had been no unscrupulous Healers who would take advantage of such blind trust.

Panicked by the seriousness of Adia's condition, Nadiwani snapped, "Khon'Tor, I do not have time to debate this!"

Khon'Tor could ill afford to appear uncaring, so he turned to Acaraho and said, "Do whatever has to be done. With the lock-down completed and nearly everyone inside, I will take care of whatever else comes up. I will also send Mapiya and Haiwee to help with the Waschini's care." He then turned and went, leaving Acaraho with his assignment.

Acaraho, who normally stood perfectly still, shifted his weight and looked over at Is'Taqa.

"Nadiwani, could not a female be more appropriately provided?" asked Is'Taqa.

"I know this is unconventional by all the normal standards of our people. But Adia is going to die if we do not get her body temperature up, and fast. A female does not have the muscle mass of a man, not even among our people. And muscle mass is what produces body heat. And right now, body heat, as much as we can get, is what she needs. I understand what I am asking of Acaraho. If there were any other way, I would not put him in this position." And with that, all concerns about protocol and propriety were taken off the table.

Is'Taqa sighed and looked apologetically at Acaraho.

"I will go, and I will return with Ithua. Adia is too important to both our tribe and yours. You will not have to handle this alone, Nadiwani," said Is'Taqa. "I will be back as soon as I can."

"Thank you, Is'Taqa. But please be mindful of the Waschini riders," she warned.

"The Waschini riders?" Is'Taqa was confused.

"Were you not there today when Akule arrived with the message from Khon'Tor?" she asked.

"No, I must already have been on the way here with the wrappings and furs."

"Khon'Tor dispatched Akule to warn you and Chief Ogima," explained Acaraho. "We received word from the High Council that there is a complement of Waschini riders passing through during the next few days. Khon'Tor ordered a lock-down, and everyone was brought inside."

"Thank you. I will be careful returning home, and Ithua and I will stay undercover and take an indirect path," replied Is'Taqa, and he left the room.

Despite Nadiwani's speech, Acaraho was confident she had no real understanding of his rising discomfort over what she was asking him to do. She signaled him to come over to where he had laid Adia on her sleeping mat.

"I need you to lie down next to her, up against her back, as close as you can get," she directed.

Acaraho lowered himself and stretched out on the sleeping mat behind Adia.

"Closer," directed Nadiwani. "Now, carefully pull her over and partially onto you until as much of her body surface is resting on yours as possible."

Acaraho did as he was told. He looked up at Nadiwani when he felt how cold Adia was. She needed him—needed his body heat at least—and he was now grateful he had been chosen and not some other male.

Nadiwani suggested a few adjustments, then when Adia was in as much contact with him as possible, pulled the wraps up over them. She went to the bundle Acaraho's guard had been carrying and had set down in the corner. She found the fur blankets Is'Taqa had brought and piled them on top too.

Though Nadiwani had given her explanation of this procedure matter-of-factly and had executed her directions to Acaraho in an utterly professional manner, he was finding nothing clinical about this experience whatsoever.

The People had not been involved in a serious battle in generations, but they still passed down and practiced what would be called military disciplines.

Fortunately, Acaraho had been trained in several techniques on how to sever his thoughts from what his body was experiencing, and he employed every one he could remember, ordered as he had been to lie here with the People's Healer pressed up against him. The mind-body practices were meant to manage fear and overwhelming pain, but Acaraho was grateful they worked with other body signals as well.

As Acaraho lay tortured next to Adia, Nadiwani prepared everything she could think of that might help boost Adia's natural healing responses. The next day would be critical.

Acaraho was also grateful that Nadiwani never left the room. Had she started to do so, he would have spoken up and demanded that she not. Only Nadiwani's current, uninterrupted presence in the room could protect him from any later accusations of impropriety. He was deeply grateful to the Great Spirit that Khon'Tor and Is'Taqa both knew what Nadiwani had asked him to do, and that the two females who had been allowed to assist Adia in caring for Oh'Dar would be coming and going as well.

Over the next few hours, Acaraho was away from Adia only for the briefest periods necessary. Despite his discomfiting role, at least he could feel her breathing and occasionally stirring, which told him she was still alive.

He prayed to the Great Spirit for Adia to recover,

but he also prayed she would not wake up while he was still pressed up against her, his arms wrapped around her, keeping her tight against his body.

◯

Is'Taqa made it back to his village in record time. He found his sister, and with both reluctance and difficulty told her what he had witnessed.

"I believe you, brother, but at the same time I can *not* believe it!"

"I understand. I am repulsed by what he did, and his crimes would be unforgivable to the People. If I had not seen it with my own eyes— And that is the problem, Ithua. If Adia survives, I will come forward. But if she does not, then accusing Khon'Tor would be to risk the generations of peace between our tribes."

Ithua agreed with him. "You are right. Every scenario, other than the one where Adia lives to come forward, would create a rift that might never be closed. More than likely, it would grow wider and wider until it turned into a serious separation of ways—maybe even confrontation."

And they both knew that in a war between his people and the Sasquatch, the Brothers would not survive.

◯

Is'Taqa returned before first light, bringing his sister, Medicine Woman of the Brothers. Ithua brought a basket of various tinctures and medicines, and Nadiwani nearly burst into tears of relief at seeing her. They greeted each other as one Healer to another, but also as friend to friend.

Ithua asked Nadiwani to tell her everything about Adia's injuries, leaving out no detail, no matter how inconsequential she thought it might be. While she explained, Ithua was relieved to hear Nadiwani had so far only attended to the head injuries.

After she was done, Ithua asked to see Adia.

Nadiwani brought her over to the sleeping area in the back of the room and pointed to where Adia lay, nestled up snugly against Acaraho, under a pile of all the covers they could find.

Is'Taqa had brought the largest wolf skin Nadiwani had ever seen in her life, and he laid it down, significantly adding to the insulating properties of the pile already covering them.

Ithua looked down at the arrangement with Adia cradled up against the muscular figure of Acaraho. She nodded and turned to Nadiwani with approval, "Good. You did well. If she lives, it will be because of what you did to bring up her core temperature." Ithua, too, saw this purely as a medical procedure and was oblivious to the indelicate position in which Nadiwani had put Acaraho.

"How long has she been on her back?" the Medicine Woman asked. "I think we should turn her over;

that will bring more of her body in contact with Acaraho," she added, matter-of-factly.

They rolled Adia over, so she was lying front to front against Acaraho with her head resting on his chest, and replaced the covers. The two males looked at each other. Is'Taqa almost chuckled at the look of desperation in Acaraho's eyes.

Satisfied that this was a better position for Adia, Nadiwani and Ithua returned to their conversation. By the way in which they were openly discussing the Healer's injuries, it seemed to Is'Taqa that Nadiwani did not know what Khon'Tor had done to Adia. He knew Ithua would tend to Adia's needs and wounds in private and ensure they were not discovered if they had not already been.

Is'Taqa shook his head, feeling nothing but sympathy for the High Protector's suffering. After a while, he left Acaraho to his agony, certain that if the male could have left his body, he would have.

In the Healer's Quarters, Ithua was taking charge. "Nadiwani, let me tend to Adia for a while. You need to rest. I promise I will call you if anything changes," she said.

Nadiwani nodded and slipped away to her quarters. Her exhaustion overrode her worry for her friend, and she was asleep within moments.

CHAPTER 14

That morning, after all the activity had slowed down, Akule headed back to his sleeping area, lost in thought with his head down and his brows furrowed.

It was improper that Khon'Tor told me to tell no one, not even the High Protector. He left alone to look for the Healer when he should have taken a guard with him. And he had me relieve the guard outside the Great Entrance, which means I am the only one who knows he went after her. Maybe I am the only one who knows she left Kthama.

Akule did not want to believe Khon'Tor had caused Adia's injuries. He wanted to believe that at worst there had been a misunderstanding. Everyone knew there was tension between them. Those who had witnessed Khon'Tor initiate the Rah-hora had seen the angry looks, the bristling challenging postures, had heard Adia unnecessarily slam her palm up against his to seal the agreement.

And then there was the matter of the agreement itself. The Rah-hora was reserved for the most severe issues, and the stakes were high for the parties on each side. The fact that Khon'Tor had initiated Rah-hora and Adia had accepted it underscored the serious problems between them, though no one knew what these were.

Perhaps there was a disagreement, and she accidentally fell and hit her head on the rocks.

And he left her there to die.

Or perhaps they had an argument that ended in a tussle, and she fell and accidentally hit her head.

And he left her there to die.

No matter how I try to explain it, there is no acceptable explanation that excuses Khon'Tor's behavior. At best Khon'Tor is a coward for leaving her there knowing she was hurt. At worst? At worst he is a monster, no better than the Waschini.

The only way Khon'Tor can be innocent is if there was a series of unbelievable circumstances which make it seem he was involved when he truly had nothing to do with it. If Adia slipped and fell all by herself and was too injured or sick to return for help. And if no one left her there to die, so it is nobody's fault, just a tragic accident.

Then Akule went over the other facts of the evening.

I was the one who reported to Khon'Tor that Adia had

left the cave. I was the one who told Khon'Tor where to look for her. I was the one Khon'Tor ordered to relieve the guard at the entrance. I am the only one who knows Khon'Tor went after Adia. And I am the only one who knows Khon'Tor returned just before Is'Taqa came for help.

Was it an accident, and that will be the end of it? I do not believe that, and I doubt anyone else would either if they knew what I do.

If Khon'Tor was innocent, Akule had nothing to fear. If the Leader was to any extent guilty, there were three possible outcomes. Khon'Tor would come to him and try to explain, hoping for Akule's forgiveness and voluntary silence. Or Khon'Tor would come to him and make a deal for his silence. Or Khon'Tor would find a way to dispose of him entirely. If his thinking was right, one of these would happen fairly soon.

Akule was worried for his life.

❂

At the other end of Kthama, Khon'Tor paced back and forth, running similar scenarios through his head. Not having any idea if Hakani was still in their quarters, and with everything on his mind, he was not going there. Instead, he went to one of the smaller chambers used as meeting rooms and holed up. He needed time and privacy.

Only two people know I am responsible for Adia's

injuries—Adia and I. My problem becomes serious only if Adia survives. And it is too early to tell that.

As for the other events of that evening, Akule, of everyone, knows the most. Akule was the one who told me Adia had left Kthama, Akule was the one who told me where to find her, Akule knows I left Kthama. He knows I returned just before Is'Taqa arrived to say he had found Adia and she was injured. None of it confirms my guilt, but none of it would help my case either, should his suspicions be raised.

For a moment, Khon'Tor thought seriously about killing Akule. But two traumatic events so close together would be entirely too suspicious. It would not be long before news of Adia's injury spread all over the community, and Hakani had been in their quarters when Akule pounded on the door in a state of extreme distress. She knew Khon'Tor and Akule had left together. Akule had relieved the guard scheduled to be at the entrance and was, therefore, guarding it when Is'Taqa arrived and led them to Adia. Akule did not have the authority to give orders to another guard, so the command had to come from either Acaraho or Khon'Tor, and it would not take long for someone to learn it had not come from Acaraho.

As more and more pieces started to surface, someone was bound to put them together. Khon'Tor and Akule, Akule and Khon'Tor. There were too many incidents tying them together.

No, it would be just too convenient if something

happened to Akule. So if I am not going to kill him, I need to find out if he suspects I harmed Adia or if he believes it was an accident.

If Akule suspected him, then Khon'Tor had to determine whether Akule could be *persuaded* to cover it up, or if he was one of those who would feel the need to clear his conscience by telling others what had happened.

Some people can keep a secret; some cannot. Which one is Akule? Khon'Tor would not be able to sleep until he found out.

Akule had two things going for him. One was that he had also not slept the previous night and had used the time to go over every possible strategy should Khon'Tor approach him. The second was that he knew how to think things through logically.

Akule decided that innocent people would not worry about the coincidences. *An innocent male, knowing his innocence, would not try to find out if others thought he was innocent. He would assume they knew he was innocent because there was no thought of guilt in his own mind.*

A guilty male, on the other hand, knowing his guilt would be looking anxiously over his shoulder to see if others were uncovering the signs of that guilt—signs he knew were there to be found because he had been present when they happened.

If Khon'Tor came to him, Akule would know the Leader had played some part in Adia's injury. How much of a role Khon'Tor had played—whether he simply knew about it and had kept quiet, or whether he had been actively involved—was what Akule would then have to figure out.

Akule was right—it did not take long for Khon'Tor to make a move.

While Akule was trudging along the cool rock floor to his assigned post, Khon'Tor appeared and began walking alongside him.

As they approached the meeting room where the Leader had spent the night, Khon'Tor asked Akule to step in for a moment.

Once in the rock-walled room, never one to be bothered with niceties, Khon'Tor got right to the point.

"The People are going to be in an uproar today when they find out what happened to Adia. And before all the commotion starts, I wanted to take a moment to thank you for your help last night."

"You do not have to thank me, Adoeete, I was just fulfilling my duties," Akule replied.

Other than the respectful term the guard used instead of addressing him by name, Khon'Tor found Akule's response noncommittal.

"No, you went above and beyond when you came

to my quarters to tell me the Healer had left. Though I was not successful in finding her, I appreciate that you came to me so promptly. Who knows, perhaps if I could have found her myself, I could have stopped her from getting hurt. I am just sorry I was not successful," Khon'Tor said.

"I do not mean to be indelicate, Adoeete, but it was obvious when I came to your door that I interrupted something *important* between you and your mate," said Akule.

Important? Akule thinks he interrupted a passionate exchange between Hakani and me. I did not think the enraged state I was in might be interpreted as arousal. Or that I was angry with him for interrupting us at an inconvenient moment. He did glance past me. She was lying on my bed. I can see how he might have taken it that way—

Akule was continuing. "You gave up your plans for the evening and went to try and find the Healer. No one would ask for more than that from a Leader, to sacrifice his personal interests for one of his people who might be in need."

Again, Akule's euphemisms were not lost on Khon'Tor. It appeared the watcher had dismissed his actions as those of a dedicated Leader going beyond the call of duty.

"Have you heard anything more about the Healer's condition, Adoeete?" asked Akule.

"No, I have not," said Khon'Tor. "I was on my way there next. Thank you, Akule. Last night was very taxing for everyone. I hope you got some rest for yourself."

Akule nodded, acknowledging that the conversation had ended. Khon'Tor dismissed him from the room and sat for a moment.

He would have liked to press Akule further. But the watcher's misinterpretation of Khon'Tor's rage toward Hakani had thrown the Leader off-stride. *Maybe it was the only thing that left an impression on Akule. It is possible he did not see any further than the surface and took it all at face value. A concerned Leader had gone out looking for one of his people after being told she might be in trouble.*

Khon'Tor sat there, realizing he did not know any more than he had the night before. *Either Akule honestly does not suspect me of any wrongdoing—or he is smarter than he looks.*

Hakani had waited nervously all evening for Khon'Tor to come back. All her planning and manipulation had come to nothing because of the watcher pounding on the door just when Khon'Tor was about to break.

She paced around their quarters. *I played my best hand. I cannot think of another way to make him so angry again. He will not fall for another set-up.*

Hakani knew that without being in a mad rage, Khon'Tor would never commit such a crime against her or anyone else for that matter. In all the years of his leadership, there had never been a charge or even an accusation of misconduct against him. He was high tempered but strong-willed, and he never lost control of his actions.

She had thought it all out carefully. When she had signaled her desire to mate with him, she was reassured to feel his response to her. But she had to time her rejection of him precisely; if she had waited too long, she would have been committed to the act, and she had no intention of allowing him that satisfaction.

However, his taking of her Without Her Consent was never Hakani's plan. Khon'Tor thought he had won because he had stopped himself in time, but for Hakani the game had only begun. She was not going to leave her plan to discredit him and strip him of his honor to a 'he said, or she said' accusation between an estranged pair. She knew Khon'Tor would threaten Bak'tah-Awhidi to set her aside and take a second mate, and she was ready with the felling blow. In telling Khon'Tor she was with offspring, but that it was not his, she had trumped his last move. Hakani had intended to inflame him to the point of committing an act for which there would be no forgiveness.

He had no idea I was lying about being with offspring! I never mated with another male. I know better than to offer myself to anyone else. Despite the rise and fall of his favor, he is still the Leader, and out of respect for him, no male would touch me. But he does not know that. At that point, she had thought she could see his mind snap and she had prepared herself, hoping that in his rage, he would not kill her.

Hakani remembered looking up at Khon'Tor as he stood over her with blood lust burning in his eyes and realized he probably would have killed her had the watcher not come to their quarters at just that moment. She wondered if in some ways the interruption had not been for the best. She had underestimated the extent of his anger. Unable to stand being isolated in their quarters any longer, she left and went to the Great Chamber.

Even as she approached the room, she could feel the electrified atmosphere. Hakani had lost favor with the People, so they did not actively seek contact with her, but if she approached them, they would never be rude enough to shun her completely either. So when she walked up to a group to hear what was going on, several of them stepped back so she could join their circle.

The only thing anyone seemed to know was that the Healer had been hurt, possibly very seriously, in some kind of fall. Nadiwani and the Brothers' Medicine Woman, Ithua, were caring for her. That Ithua was there was immediate cause for speculation, but that seemed to be all anyone knew.

What Hakani knew and none of the others did, was that the previous evening, someone had come to the Leader's Quarters, frantically pounding on the door over some obviously urgent matter. And that Khon'Tor had left with him and not returned to their quarters for the rest of the night. Hakani was sure it had to be related to Adia's accident.

She looked around the expansive room. Though it was teeming with bodies, Khon'Tor was always easy to spot. If his extreme height did not give him away, his crown of silver hair did. Not finding him, she wondered where he could be.

Khon'Tor was still sitting in the same chamber in which he had just finished his conversation with Akule. But he needed an update on Adia's status, so he headed in that direction.

When he arrived, he asked the guard to let Nadiwani know he was there—even the Leader had to have permission to enter the Healer's Quarters. While he was waiting, he made it a point to listen to the tone of the conversation. He had been informed that Ithua had arrived to help, and she and Nadiwani were speaking calmly. He listened carefully, so he would notice any shift when his arrival was announced. It would not tell him much, but it might be a clue as to whether they had discovered there was more to her injuries than the blow to her head. If they had, they might stop talking when he appeared.

Even in his blind rage, Khon'Tor had known Adia was a maiden and that he was very likely hurting her seriously in his assault. At the time, he had not cared; if anything, it led to much of his satisfaction. Now he realized that where otherwise they might not have discovered the violation, there would be physical evidence of the force to which, in his fury, he had subjected Adia. Evidence that might lead them to the discovery. And there would be no other explanation than the obvious for how *those* injuries had come about.

Khon'Tor stepped into the room. The two females looked up, and Nadiwani nodded at him in acknowledgment. She told him it was still touch and go, and that they were now waiting to see if Ithua's medicines and Acaraho's body heat would be enough to turn her condition in the right direction.

"Do you still need his services?" asked Khon'Tor, looking over at Acaraho. He was wondering what the High Protector had overheard during all this time in the room with them and was anxious for a report.

"A little while longer until she is out of the woods."

As they were standing there, Adia started to come around and made a little sound. Nadiwani and Ithua went immediately to her.

Unfortunately, she did not stay awake long enough to notice Khon'Tor and slipped back into unconsciousness.

"Do you still have need of Acaraho's services?" Khon'Tor asked again.

Nadiwani and Ithua exchanged a few words, and they went back to Adia.

Nadiwani touched Adia's face, checking for warmth. "There is no longer any sign of fever, and her skin feels warm to the touch. But I retain the right to have Acaraho back, should Adia's body temperature drop in the slightest," she told him firmly.

When Adia had started stirring, and Nadiwani came over with Ithua to check her, Acaraho took advantage of the opportunity to get up. He eased Adia off him and slipped from the sleeping mat. He did not want her waking up and finding herself lying in bed in his arms. Acaraho locked his eyes on Adia's every movement as she was waking up. He was waiting for her to notice Khon'Tor, standing there in the room. At the same time, he was also watching Khon'Tor.

If Khon'Tor had anything to do with Adia being hurt, I will see it in his reaction and hers when she first notices him. Between the two of them, someone's response will tell me what I need to know.

When Khon'Tor asked if the High Protector could be relieved of his duty, Acaraho was both grateful and not; without being constantly in the room, the odds were that he would not be present when she woke. And he needed to be there to witness that unguarded moment between her and

Khon'Tor. And as long as Acaraho was in the room, he was aware of Adia's condition at all times. Lastly, no one was better prepared or better able to protect her than he was.

Knowing Khon'Tor, Acaraho was sure the Leader wanted to find out what had been overhead in the room over the past day.

Khon'Tor had plans, but so did Acaraho and none of his included being taken away from Adia.

"Come with me, Acaraho," said Khon'Tor. Then, turning to Ithua and Nadiwani, he added, "If her condition changes, send word to me immediately. Thank you." He started to walk away, expecting the High Protector to follow him.

Acaraho did not want to play this card yet, but he needed a way to stay with Ithua, Nadiwani, and Adia.

Without moving from his current position, he said, "Adoeete, may I make the point that there is still a threat to the Healer aside from her injuries."

"I do not know what you mean, Acaraho. I doubt Hakani would try anything right now, and there are two females with her at all times," replied Khon'Tor.

"I was not referring to your mate, Khon'Tor," answered Acaraho, this time intentionally addressing Khon'Tor by name instead of the more formal title, Adoeete.

His eyes locked on Khon'Tor for any reaction to his next statement, "It is possible what happened to the Healer was not an accident," and he delivered his first blow to Khon'Tor's protective veneer.

There it was.

Khon'Tor blinked.

With the slightest of motions, he just gave himself away. So Khon'Tor did play a role in Adia's injuries. The next questions are, what was his role, and to what extent —if any—was he responsible for those injuries?

"Can another take your place here?" asked Khon'Tor.

"Awan is my best guard, and Adia managed to trick him long enough to leave the protection of Kthama," was Acaraho's reply. "Also, should her condition take a turn for the worse, they may need my services again," he added.

The Leader's chance to learn anything from Acaraho's stint in the Healer's Quarters evaporated before him.

Khon'Tor *cannot fight me too hard on this, or it will be obvious he is not concerned for the Healer's safety.*

"Very well," replied Khon'Tor. "I bow to your judgment."

To Acaraho, that was the second tell regarding Khon'Tor's involvement. Though Acaraho held the second-highest command position, Khon'Tor would never give up any of his status over anyone, however thin his edge. He would not under any circumstances show any subservience, even to Acaraho. His statements, accompanied by a slight nod in Acaraho's direction, were meant to flatter the High Protector and to win his favor.

The score was now two for two, in favor of Khon'-Tor's guilt.

The Leader continued on his way, and Acaraho remained in the Healer's Quarters.

◑

Days passed. Khon'Tor received word that the Waschini party had passed through the People's territory and out at its farthest borders without incident. He called another general assembly and shared that the threat had passed, but announced he was leaving the watchers in place.

◑

Adia awoke fully on the morning of the third day following her injury. She was piled under an enormous weight of blankets, and everything everywhere seemed to hurt. A shadow of alarm went through her when she first noticed the weight of the furs, but it faded, and then they became a comfort. She raised her head and realized she was somehow back in her quarters, and she recognized the voices of Nadiwani and Ithua. She felt safe and so relieved that someone had found her and brought her back.

Once she knew where she was and that she was safe, Adia lay still for a while, collecting her thoughts and trying to remember what had happened. She wanted some time to think for herself before all the questions started.

She remembered Khon'Tor telling everyone about the Waschini riding party coming through, and his order that no one could leave.

Why did I have to go and dig up the locket? What was I thinking? That was foolish. I must have been sick and not thinking straight. She remembered tricking Awan and escaping Kthama through the water-return stream in the females' bathing area.

She had found the locket she had buried in its little pouch and was on her way back when Khon'Tor was suddenly blocking her way. She could tell he was very angry. Adia was not sure what happened next, but the last few things she remembered were Khon'Tor yelling at her and hitting her, followed by her head exploding and her body slamming hard onto the cold, snow-covered ground. After that, she remembered, a struggle to remain conscious. She had slipped in and out, finally losing the battle but not before she felt Khon'Tor's tremendous weight almost crushing her and then a violent pain she had never imagined and could not recognize as anything she had experienced before.

As she remembered all of this, the horror of what had happened hit her full force. She choked back a sob, trying to get her reactions under control.

Khon'Tor had intentionally hit her, knocked her to the ground, and left her there to die. But in addition to all that, he had committed an unspeakable act against her. Her mind could not accept it. Attacking her—hitting a female—was bad enough. But she could not fathom that he would violate her. It was not only against one of the laws of the People, but it was also one of their most sacred. Worse yet, she was a maiden and a Healer. *Was*, thought Adia to herself. She had never been paired, but she understood full well the cause of the pain still throbbing through her center.

A terrifying thought hit her. *Who tended to me? Was it Ithua? Nadiwani? Do they realize what was done to me? I am not ready to face them.*

She quietly rolled over, pulled the skins up over her, and retreated into herself. *Whatever awful things I thought of Khon'Tor in the past, I never thought him capable of this. I cannot imagine why he did something so terrible. I have defied him before. I know I should not have left, but what was so dreadful about me slipping out that it would invoke such a brutal and irrational response?*

Adia needed time to let her feelings flow, to grieve, to let the tears out. *I need time to figure out what to do. They are going to have questions I am not yet prepared to answer.*

When Adia felt she was finally ready to make it known that she was awake, she rolled over and partially sat up. It took only seconds for Nadiwani and Ithua to notice, and only a few more before both were at her side.

Nadiwani sat down on the edge of the sleeping

mat next to Adia and took her hand, smiling that her friend was finally fully awake. Ithua went about checking Adia's signs and reassuring herself the Healer was finally out of the woods.

As Acaraho had predicted, Khon'Tor was not in the room when Adia came around. But Acaraho was there, and he was grateful for that.

Standing against the wall at his usual post, it was all he could do not to rush over to her side as well.

To krell with it. I have been used as a heated sleeping mat for that female, in her own bed no less. I think protocol can take this little hit. And with that, he stepped away from where he usually stood and went over to join them.

Adia looked up as Acaraho came over, this time not avoiding eye contact. She immediately felt safer, knowing he was nearby.

"How do you feel, Adia?" asked Nadiwani, "Please tell me; what hurts and where?"

"Everything and everywhere," was her reply.

Nadiwani sighed, letting the matter go because she was sure the clinical aspects of Adia's injuries were not at the top of the Healer's mind.

"Adia," this time Acaraho spoke. This was only

the second time he had ever addressed her directly. Adia looked up at him, transfixed, wanting never to break eye contact.

"What do you remember about how you got hurt? Can you tell me what happened?" he asked. She thought she detected tenderness in his voice.

Adia had prepared for this question as she was lying there trying to remember what had happened.

She knew the consequences for Khon'Tor would be severe. But once made public the effects of what he had done to her would rock the foundations of their community and inflict immeasurable suffering on all the People. At a time when they needed faith and trust in their leadership to face the challenges that were ahead for them, to find out what Khon'Tor was capable of could shatter the framework of their society.

This is bigger than my injuries. I can deal with those myself privately. But I am not ready to deal with the chaos and even civil war that might well result from this. I need more time.

Adia looked up at Acaraho, and because it broke her heart to withhold anything from him, she could not maintain eye contact and looked down before answering him.

"I am not sure. It is all very fuzzy. I remember hitting the ground, and my head exploding with pain," she said. "I remember feeling so very tired and so cold. And I remember being carried," she continued. Technically, this was all true.

"And then I remember a feeling of such comfort and warmth. Safety. Protection, really— I do not remember why. And then I woke up a little while ago," she added.

Adia knew someone with a head injury could often lose memory—sometimes only temporarily, sometimes permanently. She knew Nadiwani and Ithua also knew this, and she was counting on them to speak up now.

"Do not worry about it, Adia," said Nadiwani. "Sometimes, it takes a while for the memories to return. Just rest and let me get you something to eat. You have not eaten in days."

And then Adia could stand it no longer. She had to know what they knew.

"My head is splitting; what happened?" she asked.

So Nadiwani told her the story of how Is'Taqa found her while bringing the pelts and wrappings for Oh'Dar, and that he ran to Kthama and brought back help.

"Acaraho was the one who carried you back," she said. Adia wondered if his carrying her was the comfort and warmth she remembered. But it seemed to have lasted far longer than the distance between there and home.

Nadiwani added, "We have been doing everything we can to help you get better. You took a serious blow to your head and had a fever. I think you were perhaps sick before you even left Kthama."

Adia touched Nadiwani's fingers and then reached out and took Ithua's hand, looking up into her eyes. The Medicine Woman just nodded and squeezed her hand back. For a Medicine Woman to leave her tribe to help another was an extraordinary sacrifice and risk. Adia hoped Ithua could feel her gratitude and vowed she would someday repay this incredible debt.

So far, Nadiwani has only mentioned my head injury and fever. There was no mention of anything or anyone else. I know Nadiwani; if she discovered the truth, she would not be able to contain it.

It must have been Ithua who tended to me then. If she noticed, she would not say anything except to me personally. Other than that, everyone thinks it was an accident and will go on thinking that as long as I do not say otherwise.

Adia felt an immediate sense of relief. For now, she had time to figure out how to respond to what Khon'Tor had done to her.

❂

Acaraho had duly noted that Adia broke eye contact with him before she answered his questions about what had happened and what she remembered. He also realized she had given only the most mundane, neutral answers. There was not one thing she had said that told them any more than they already knew.

There should have been at least some pieces of new information in her answer, but there was not one. Adia was holding back, but why?

❂

As requested, Nadiwani sent word to Khon'Tor that Adia had come around. Khon'Tor received the message and dismissed the messenger. He sat unmoving for a while, a cold knot in the pit of his stomach. That a complement of guards had not come to arrest him meant she had not told them what he did. But why not? Why would she not tell them what he had done to her?

He knew he would have to go to her directly to find out.

❂

Each day, Adia became a little stronger. She was able to hold and care for Oh'Dar. Her headaches were getting better. Her other minor cuts and scrapes, treated early on by Nadiwani, had all healed. Satisfied with Adia's progress, Ithua and Is'Taqa returned to their tribe of the Brothers. Adia remembered to give them the basket of gifts she had collected in return for the skins and wrappings they had brought for Oh'Dar against the cold weather that was now upon them.

It had been three days since Khon'Tor was notified that Adia was awake. He knew it had gone on too long, not going to see her before now. He could not let another day go by. Because he needed permission to enter the Healer's Quarters, he let them know he was on his way.

Adia had been told that Khon'Tor was coming to see her. *The Leader of the People; the powerful, towering male who angrily struck me to the ground, then violated me in my helpless and injured state, and afterward walked away, leaving me to die, is coming to visit me to see how I am doing. How thoughtful.*

She thought she had prepared herself for this, but now the moment was upon her, Adia was not sure she was ready.

She had also thought many times about telling the others what he had done. She did not think they would disbelieve her. But she could not decide if the call for justice to be served was worth the terrible consequences that would ensue from revealing Khon'Tor's crimes.

Adia needed to talk to Khon'Tor alone. But she would have to do so under different circumstances—not in her quarters with Nadiwani, Oh'Dar, and

Acaraho around. What must happen must happen between the two of them alone.

Adia prepared herself for his entrance, practicing her most nonchalant affect. If she was going to follow through on the story that she did not remember what had happened, she had to set her mind to react as if he was nothing more than the Leader of the People—not the monster she now knew him to be.

The guard announced Khon'Tor's arrival, and Adia could feel Acaraho watching both of them intently. She did not know whether he suspected something; he might simply be feeling protective of her after what she had been through. She believed they were convinced that she had memory only of what she had already told them. Now Adia had to see if she could convince Khon'Tor of the same.

Adia and Nadiwani had been at the work table where Nadiwani was sharing with the Healer what she had learned from Ithua in administering to Adia's needs.

Khon'Tor spoke first. "I am pleased to see you have recovered," he said.

Liar, thought Adia, almost sneering. She was glad she had not quite lost control. Khon'Tor might be heartless and ruthless and perhaps a monster, but he was no fool, and he would be paying attention to everything she said and did. He would be evaluating every inflection of her voice, every eye movement. She knew the greatest risk was when she made eye contact with him. She was not sure if he knew she was claiming to remember hardly anything, but he would realize that no accusations had been brought because no one had come pounding at his door.

Their entire society had been shaken by the few instances in the People's history when charges of misconduct were leveled against someone in a position of high authority. Violations of the laws were usually handled by the internal structure within each community. They were decided through discussion of the facts between the Leader, the Healer, and the Leader's mate as Third Rank. At their discretion, other authorities could be brought in to counsel them, such as those in the position held by Acaraho. The ultimate seat of power. however, rested in the Leader's hands and the final justice was his alone to decide.

In the rare case that an issue involved any of the ruling ranks, the High Council would be brought in because judgment over those situations had to be taken to a seat of power outside of the community itself. Above all the ranks within the community, including the Leader himself, was the High Council —a combination of Leaders and Chiefs from the tribes in the area who came together to discuss matters of mutual concern. So the fact that Khon'Tor was left to go about his business would have told him she had revealed nothing of what he did to her. The question was, why had she not? Adia knew Khon'Tor was there to find out the answer.

She had every intention of confronting Khon'Tor

about what he had done, but it would not be here, not in front of others. She could not afford to lose control of what happened next, and if others found out, it would unleash unbearable pandemonium.

The only people in the room, besides herself and Khon'Tor, were Nadiwani and Acaraho. Adia did not care if she fooled Khon'Tor right now with her story of amnesia, but she did care that she continued to fool them.

Adia took the plunge, met Khon'Tor's gaze, and said, "I am coming along, thanks to the care of Nadiwani and Ithua. Thank you for asking."

Khon'Tor could not wait any longer. Knowing he was at huge risk of tipping his hand, he still had to ask, "What happened to you? Do you remember?"

Acaraho was watching as Khon'Tor almost imperceptibly took a breath and held it while he waited for Adia to answer.

"I cannot say," she replied, trying to walk as close to the truth as possible. "A lot of what happened is a blur. I am just thankful Is'Taqa found me in time."

Khon'Tor knew she certainly would not accuse him in this setting. He knew that if she were going to bring accusations against him, it would be through the formal process of contacting the High Council. He only hoped that through what she did say he would get more information than he currently had—

which was basically nothing. But now he knew no more than he had when he arrived.

○

Adia's noncommittal answers were not lost on Acaraho.

Once again, he thought, *answering without providing any real information. I am convinced that Adia is pretending she does not remember.*

And Khon'Tor held his breath after he asked her if she remembered what had happened. And instead of asking the more obvious question in keeping with his demand for unwavering obedience—Why did you leave Kthama when I had forbidden it?—*he asked if she remembered.*

Khon'Tor did not have to ask why she was out there because he already knew. Perhaps that was the reason for their fight—or part of it. Khon'Tor asked a question to which he did not know the answer: what did she remember?

Acaraho had no more doubt that whatever had happened to Adia, Khon'Tor had played a part in it. His list of unanswered questions was long, the most important being, *Was Khon'Tor the one to inflict Adia's injuries?*

○

Khon'Tor had other problems besides the huge inconvenience of Adia's survival. One of his other problems was his mate, who unfortunately was also alive and well. The last time he had seen Hakani, he was towering over her as she lay in his bed—just seconds away from eviscerating her.

Whatever she had been doing since that night, he knew it would not be for his benefit.

There was also still the matter of Akule, to whom Khon'Tor in truth probably owed a great debt, as it was Akule who had unknowingly stopped him from killing Hakani.

Had Akule not pounded on the door at just the moment he did, I would have violently and savagely ended Hakani's life. No staging could have covered that up, he thought.

Reflecting on how close he had come to killing Hakani, Khon'Tor realized how out of his mind he had been that night. And yes, he would normally have been angry with Adia for leaving Kthama, but he would not have reacted in the crazed, explosive manner he did. He realized his unrelieved rage at Hakani had been redirected and unleashed on Adia. Otherwise, he would never have allowed himself to lose control and hit a female, let alone— And he forced himself to leave that thought unfinished, not wanting to revisit just then what he had done to her afterward.

CHAPTER 15

apiya and Haiwee, who were caring for Oh'Dar, were also providing any assistance they could to Nadiwani. Nadiwani regularly sent them back to the community with ongoing updates about Adia's progress. When the news came that Adia had regained consciousness and was expected to make a full recovery, the energy in the population changed from concerned to jubilant.

Hakani did not particularly care whether Adia lived or died—neither changed the fact that Adia had been Khon'Tor's First Choice all along. Though Hakani would probably have derived some satisfaction from Adia's death, she was more interested in punishing Khon'Tor.

I felt so honored when he selected me as his mate. I pictured a rewarding lifetime at his side. I thought I would be his counsel and his support, his Third Rank, enjoying the respect of the People.

But when Hakani learned Khon'Tor had only selected her by default, all her dreams turned to humiliation. And that humiliation had turned to hatred—hatred that was kept alive by the constant presence of Adia, his First Choice, in their day-to-day lives.

Hakani was not sure what repercussions there would be for what she had done. She was not sure what else he could do to her. He had already nullified her position of leadership in the People's eyes; he had cut her off from participating in any role as his mate, and he had evicted her from his sleeping area—a fact which had caused her tremendous humiliation.

Her only satisfaction was that he left believing she was carrying another man's offspring. And that this would be a great source of torment for him for as long as she could carry out the ruse. She knew that within a few months, she would have to drop the pretense as it would be obvious she was not with offspring. But in the meantime, she was going to leverage it for all she could.

Hakani had thought through her moves very carefully and designed each step, so she had Khon'Tor beat, regardless of which way the evening went.

After leading him on and at the very last second withdrawing her consent, if he had not been able to control himself and had mated her against her will, she would have won. And as an added bonus, there would also be a chance he might have seeded her.

If it had gone that way, she would not have played the card about carrying another man's offspring. She would have waited and hoped she might be seeded, solving the problem of her obligation to produce him an heir.

But he had stopped himself and then done exactly what she knew he would; he had stated he would go to the High Council and invoke his right to select a second mate. One who would succeed where she had failed.

It was then she had played her trump card. There would be no need for a second mate; she would produce an offspring, and the fact that it would not be his was inconsequential. She would fulfill her obligation.

She knew Khon'Tor would be trapped. His pride would force him to claim the offspring rather than have anyone know she had betrayed him.

And to be forced to raise another man's offspring, and have that offspring become Leader someday, would eat away at him every day—much the same as seeing Adia ate away at Hakani every day.

She had counted on this to push him past the breaking point, and it did. If Hakani had known that the insane rage she caused him had driven him to attack Adia, she would have been very pleased indeed.

She did not know what her next move would be, but until she did, she could enjoy the fact that Khon'Tor would continue to believe for some time that she was carrying another man's offspring. And every time he looked out across the group of males he commanded, he would wonder who it was who had betrayed him. Even after Hakani had to drop the ruse, that thought would torment him the rest of his life.

Khon'Tor had not returned to his quarters since the night he almost killed Hakani. He continued to hole up in the meeting room he had taken over earlier. He missed his private retreat, but her presence ruined any solace it might have provided. And he did not want to give her another opportunity to taunt him about carrying someone else's offspring.

The thought that one of the males had betrayed him was eating at him to his core. He had pictured each one in his mind; in the end, he could not think of one male who would commit such an act. Even beyond loyalty to him, infidelity was practically unheard of among the People.

The Leadership of the People was always passed on through the bloodline. Without an heir, there was no one next in line after Khon'Tor.

Everyone will be thrilled at the news that Hakani is with offspring; I will have to put on a show. I have no proof that I did not seed the offspring. It would be my word against hers, short of whoever the father is coming forward.

Khon'Tor sat with his head in his hands. *Hakani has won. I cannot go to the High Council and claim a second mate if she is fulfilling her duty to produce one. And I now have no grounds to oust her from my quarters. It would make more sense, though, if I knew why she hates me so much.*

Khon'Tor had no solution to his problem with Akule either. The watcher knew too much about Khon'Tor's involvement in the night's events. Did Akule really think no more of what had happened than at its face value? Or did he suspect Khon'Tor but was smart enough to hide it? In the normal course of events, Khon'Tor had little interaction with the watchers, so it would be unusual for him to continue to contact Akule. For now, he had to let go of the matter. He did not want to stir up the suspicions of anyone, including the watcher himself.

I might not be able to do anything about Hakani or Akule at this point, but I do have to do something about Adia.

Adia had continued to get stronger and stronger. Her wounds had been treated and had healed. She was able to resume some care for Oh'Dar as well as some of her duties as Healer.

She continued to maintain that she did not remember much about that night. Ithua had not let on, if indeed she had recognized the other injuries. Adia knew the Medicine Woman of the Brothers would discuss it with her before mentioning it to anyone else; in Ithua's place, she would do the same.

As soon as she was able to, Adia took a long-awaited bath. Even though Ithua must have tended to her, she still wanted to wash off for herself all remembrance of what Khon'Tor had done. It was agony having to wait so long to do so. Nadiwani helped her into the bathing area and left her to her privacy.

As Adia lay enjoying the cool water, easing the remaining aches and pains, she had time to think about what she was going to do.

Outpourings of good wishes and concerned messages brought back to her from the community by Mapiya and Haiwee had raised her spirits. She found it curious, though, that there were not more questions about why she had left the cave that night. Apparently, they chalked it up to her being so sick—that in her delirium, she had simply walked out of Kthama. They certainly had not looked any deeper than that, for which she was grateful.

The furor over her injury had now died down; everyone was relieved she was going to be alright.

Adia grieved over the loss of Oh'Dar's locket, though, and the little pouch. *It must still be out there somewhere, maybe lost amid the rocks, hidden under the snow. Or maybe Khon'Tor took it. I do not know, but I have to try to find it. I will go out and look for it when I can.*

At the moment, everything seemed calm compared to the events of the past while. Adia loved the People of her community. She had always put them first. She had served them as their Healer to the best of her ability. She would do anything for them and had never meant to cause struggle and upheaval for them by bringing Oh'Dar into their midst.

Adia's thoughts turned to what she had tried not to think about all this time—that Khon'Tor had attacked her and left her for dead. She knew there was tension between them, just as there was tension between her and his mate Hakani. But for it to come to this?

Khon'Tor has been the Leader since before I came to the People as their Healer. I have seen him under various levels of stress. I have seen him lose his temper and speak out harshly. But I have never seen him threaten anyone with physical violence. Not ever. And neither are there rumors of him having done so with anyone else. He has a temper, he is strong-willed, but I would not have thought him capable of such crimes. And they were out of proportion to my crime of leaving Kthama against his decree.

The more Adia reflected on Khon'Tor's behavior,

the harder it was for her to accept that he had done this to her. In the safety and comfort of the bathing area, with no watching eyes, she released all the bottled-up pain. She let the tears flow and sobbed her heart out at what he had done to her. The feelings of helplessness and invasion, the bewilderment as to why, the anger, all came pouring out. Grief over losing her sense of safety and the loss of the sanctity of her own person flooded her and overwhelmed her. She had no one to turn to for comfort but herself, but she allowed herself that and alone, she bore witness to her pain and suffering.

Somewhere in feeling the loss of all those things, she realized she had lost something else. *No matter how angry Khon'Tor might have gotten with me in the past, no matter how much I have disagreed with him on some issues, he was still my Leader. I used to admire him. I looked up to him for strength and direction. But now I do not have even that any longer. The one person I thought was stronger than I and whom I could count on, is gone. I no longer have faith in him.*

When Adia was sad, she often thought of her father, Leader of the People of the Deep Valley, the community she'd had to leave behind when she was selected as Healer to the People of the High Rocks. She had often compared Khon'Tor's high tempered and heavy-handed style with her father's more even-tempered and measured approach. And in that comparison, she had always found fault with Khon'-Tor. Now, reflecting on the challenges facing them—

challenges the kind of which her father never had to deal with—she realized Khon'Tor's leadership style was not necessarily wrong, it was just different from that of her father.

And she now realized her father would not have been strong enough to lead the People through the storms on the horizon. It would take a strong-willed and fierce Leader to unite and direct them; someone like Khon'Tor.

When Adia came to this realization, she also came to her decision.

She would not reveal what Khon'Tor had done to her. Not because she excused it—there could never be any excuse for what he had done—and not because he did not deserve to be brought to justice. But Adia knew that if this came to light, it would divide and destroy the community. She remembered the first of the First Laws: The needs of the people come before the needs of the individual. If she put her need for justice and vengeance first, then everyone in the community would suffer.

Adia's whole body relaxed with her decision. *Living with what he did to me will be hard, but allowing what he did to destroy our community would be harder. However, I am still going to confront him about what he did. I owe myself that. But I will pick the time and place. I just have to make sure no one overhears me, and I do not want to wait much longer.*

Khon'Tor knew he could not avoid Hakani forever. She had heard where he was staying and waited to go in until she knew he would be there. Khon'Tor was both prepared and not prepared. He had no countermove against what Hakani had done. So he let her in and waited to hear what she had to say.

"Khon'Tor," she began, "I want you to call an assembly and announce that we are expecting an offspring."

"*We* are expecting an offspring?" Khon'Tor sneered.

"If you prefer, I make it known the offspring is not your doing, *Adik'Tar*, I can do that."

Khon'Tor took a deep breath. *I am tired of the battle with Hakani. Perhaps I should accept this for what it is at the moment and concentrate on my larger problem; Adia. At least there is something I can do to deal with that.*

"Alright," said Khon'Tor. "I will make the arrangements."

"I know you will be convincing, Khon'Tor," said Hakani with a smirk on her face. "It would be a shame to have everyone know another male had to step up and accomplish what the great Adoeete could not," she added.

"I am not taking the bait, Hakani. You refused me time and time again. We both know I am well able to complete the task, but you have withheld the opportunity for years."

Without the other male coming forward, it is my

word against hers. But she also cannot risk anyone knowing this is not my offspring. It is her protection against my going to the High Council and setting our pairing aside on the grounds that she has not produced my offspring. If either of us reveals the offspring is not mine, we both have much to lose.

Actually, Hakani's request for him to call a general assembly played right into what he needed to do to regain control over Adia.

Khon'Tor realized that though he did not know if Adia remembered what he had done to her, he had to proceed as if she did. There was no threat if she did not; there was every threat if she did.

He had to ensure her silence, and there was only one way he knew to do that. Two things were very dear to Adia; one was the welfare of the People, and the other was the Waschini offspring. He would fully leverage each to his end and make use of the general assembly to do this.

Word went out quickly that Khon'Tor was calling a meeting of the People. Since there had only been good news about Adia's recovery, and they had already been told the Waschini threat had passed, they anticipated that this would be a positive meeting.

Khon'Tor had to talk to Adia before the general assembly. Little did he know that while he was preparing to speak to her, she was preparing to speak to him.

Adia paced, pulling her thoughts together. She was ready to confront Khon'Tor. She needed him to know she remembered what he had done. All of it. But she was also going to tell him she would not be coming forward, while making it clear this was not in any way for his sake, but for the sake of the People. That if she could see him brought to justice without it destroying all the other people she cared about, she would. Adia knew she would not be able to evade Acaraho, so the only way she could meet with Khon'Tor was to be straight about it. Though she did not owe Acaraho an explanation, she could feel his concern for her. She had seen him watching Khon'-Tor, and she knew he had suspicions that she was not telling the truth about her failed memory.

So she knew he would be opposed to her meeting with Khon'Tor in private. But there was no way around it. What she had to say to Khon'Tor had to be said to him alone.

The afternoon of the general assembly Khon'Tor was ready to play his hand with Adia. It occurred to him that by calling everyone together, he had provided her the perfect platform to accuse him publicly if she wished. So he had to meet with her beforehand to ease his mind. If she genuinely did not remember, all was well. If she did remember, he would invoke the means necessary to compel her silence.

Khon'Tor sent word that he wanted to speak with Adia and to bring her to the room where he had set up his new center of operations. Acaraho escorted Adia to the room, but when he started to enter with her, Khon'Tor solved Adia's problem by putting his hand up to stop Acaraho at the door. "I will speak with her in private, Acaraho. Wait in the hallway outside to ensure our privacy."

Adia could see by his reaction that Acaraho was not happy. Only someone who knew him as well as she did by now would have noticed the slightest narrowing of his eyes and the clench of his jaw.

Khon'Tor directed Acaraho to a position in the hallway. Though he was still in front of the door, he was to stand several feet away. Khon'Tor knew the room was soundproof. For this very reason, it had been especially set aside for sensitive meetings. He was being extra cautious because it was Acaraho.

Khon'Tor pulled the stone slab closed, and Adia's heart beat harder at the sound of it sliding into place.

I am ready. All I need is for him to start and I will take over from there. I can safely assume that I am here because he wants to figure out if I really do not remember what happened. And if I do remember, what I am going to do about it.

I am glad to hear you should make a full recovery, Adia," said Khon'Tor walking around to face her after closing the door, then sitting down on the nearest boulder.

Adia locked her eyes on his before replying, wanting to see every flicker of reaction.

"I find that surprising to hear, Khon'Tor," she replied with ice in her voice. "You did not seem concerned for my welfare when after viciously attacking me, you left me bleeding to die in the cold snow.

"Yes, Khon'Tor. I remember. I remembered from the moment I woke up. I only needed time to deal with the shock of it, and to heal from the physical wounds you inflicted on me," she added, never taking her eyes off his.

"And the next question you want to have answered; the answer is also yes. Yes. I remember all of it. Your rage. Grabbing and hurting my wrists. Throwing me to the ground. Hitting me across the face when I got back up. Knocking me down again. And then, while I was lying helpless and defenseless, barely conscious, you mated me against my will. *Without My Consent.* And not only a maiden, Khon'-Tor, *a Healer.* You viciously attacked and violated a Healer." She spat it out.

She paused before adding the last words, slowly, for impact. "And then left her to die."

Standing quietly for a moment, Adia locked her eyes on his. He did not look away. He did not break eye contact. They stayed that way for several moments. She wanted to make sure he had heard her. And he had.

She was about to tell him about her decision not to come forward, for the sake of the People; however, he spoke first.

He got up and stood directly in front of her. "Everything you said is true. I will not deny it. I will not try to excuse it. I will not try to explain it. It is done and nothing will un-do it," he said.

Well, that is a relief. Though not an apology, at least he does not deny what he did.

Khon'Tor paused for a moment. Then, still not breaking their eye contact, he slowly raised his left hand, palm facing Adia.

Adia broke eye contact to look at his raised palm, and she frowned. *He is invoking our Rah-hora?* Her eyes flew back to his when he started speaking again.

"You are bound by our Rah-hora, an agreement you went into voluntarily. For your part, you agreed to owe me a debt that you would repay when due. You entered into this agreement aware that neither you nor I knew what the debt would be until I named it. You also agreed that if you did not fulfill my request, either your life or that offspring's would be forfeit to me." Khon'Tor never took his eyes off hers, and his voice was like steel, just as it had been the night they made the agreement.

"You have not fulfilled your part, Khon'Tor," said Adia. Her mind was racing, and she was doing her best to stay one step ahead of him now.

"I am prepared to do so tonight, Adia," said Khon'Tor. "Our agreement stands, and I am activating it now."

Though Adia understood what he was asking her to do, she needed him to say it so there could be no misunderstanding the 'favor' he was asking of her.

"State the debt, Khon'Tor," she said icily.

"Very well. You are never to reveal what happened. You are never to reveal that I struck you, or that I violated you. Or that I left you to die. You are to maintain that you do not remember the details and allow others to believe as they do now; that you slipped and fell, and hit your head. Nothing more."

Adia was satisfied that protocol had been followed and no room had been left to prevent the agreement being executed properly.

She could not believe this turn of events. She had been prepared to tell Khon'Tor that she would never reveal what he did to her. Now he was calling that in as her part of the debt. With this, she would be freed from the Rah-hora.

In another time, in another culture, another female might have shrugged off the burden of such an arrangement—after all, had Khon'Tor been held accountable for his crimes, it would be difficult for him to extract his part of the agreement. But the tradition, reverence, and sacredness of the Rah-hora were woven into the fabric of the People at a level deeper than reason could reach. Only the initiating party could release the other from the vow; barring that, both were honor-bound to fulfill it.

Adia was not going to lose this opportunity to be freed of the Rah-hora, while also assuring Oh'Dar's chance to learn Whitespeak, the language of his people—but she did not want to appear too eager to accept his terms.

"The debt you are asking for seems unfair, Khon'-Tor. You have only to provide education for Oh'Dar. I have to keep silent about two very serious crimes, crimes which would cost you your leadership and so much more," she said.

"It is the deal you agreed to. But your point is well made. I will up my side of the arrangement tonight at the general meeting." Khon'Tor's voice was emotion-less, cold, distant.

Adia paused in silence for just a moment. She increased the intensity of her stare, their eyes still locked together.

Then, as she had done before, Adia raised her hand and slammed her open palm against his, re-creating the loud resounding *crack* with which she had first accepted the agreement.

It was done.

Khon'Tor nodded at Adia and then toward the door, signaling that what needed to be said between them was accomplished. Adia turned, pushed the door aside, and left.

Acaraho had heard nothing, only the scrape of the door opening as Adia left the meeting room. He studied her as she came out, but as usual, said nothing.

They walked back in silence. Adia was deep in thought. Now Khon'Tor needed only to follow through on his part of the arrangement, and it was completed.

The moments seemed to creep by until it was finally time for the general assembly. Acaraho, Nadiwani, and Adia stood to the side of the far wall, which gave them a clear view of the front where Khon'Tor always stood.

The crowd murmured as the People speculated about the reason for this meeting. There was an excited air about the room, and all eyes fell on Khon'Tor as he and Hakani made their way through the crowd and up to the front of the enormous Great Chamber.

As was his custom, Khon'Tor raised his left hand when he was ready to speak. Once the room fell silent, he let it drop back to his side.

"Welcome. Thank you for coming. As you know, a great threat recently passed through our land. As you also know, one of our most important members, our Healer, recently had a terrible accident. I am glad to announce that she is expected to make a full recovery."

With that, the crowd turned to Adia with happy

faces.

Khon'Tor waited a moment for their attention to return to him and continued. "We are lucky to have many things to celebrate at this time. I am here with my mate, Hakani, to announce another blessing. Hakani is expecting an offspring!" he announced, causing a great commotion in the crowd. Nearly everyone had heard the rumors that they no longer shared the same sleeping area. Everyone believed they were estranged. So this was surprising news, to say the least. After much talking and turning of heads, they finally gave up a resounding cheer to congratulate the pair on this good news.

Khon'Tor waited for the cheering to die down before continuing.

"An offspring is always a blessing. An offspring is our assurance our people will continue. An offspring is innocent," said Khon'Tor. Adia realized she was holding her breath.

Pausing a moment, he then looked at Adia and said, "All offspring are born innocent. All offspring deserve a chance at a satisfying and rewarding life. I know I have told you the Waschini are monsters. Everything I hear, every report coming in to the High Council, says this is true. But I have seen the boy, Oh'Dar. You all have. He is not a monster. He is just an offspring. He can never be returned to the White Wasters, so we must give him everything he needs to become a contributing member of our community.

"For this reason, I am asking that we all embrace

this offspring as one of our own. I expect you to extend your acceptance to him as you would any offspring. I expect you to offer assistance to the Healer as you would any mother in the community. Oh'Dar is one of the People now. And as one of us, I also extend my support and protection to him."

The room was dead silent.

As Khon'Tor finished, he raised his arm, palm up, and looked at Adia. Adia raised her arm, her palm facing his, and returned his gaze. It was done. The Rah-hora was enacted.

To anyone else, this was just Khon'Tor's way of signaling that he was done speaking. But three people in the room knew something else much more important had just happened—Khon'Tor, Adia, and Acaraho.

From the platform, Hakani looked at Adia with hatred in her eyes.

It took quite a while for the assembly to break up. Well-wishers crowded around Khon'Tor and his mate and offered congratulatory back pats and hugs to Hakani. Though she had been isolated from the group, they now welcomed her back in. Others merely lingered, talking over what had just happened. The atmosphere in the chamber was filled with cheer and happiness.

Nearly all the females came over to the Healer

and offered words of support. They could not have spoken out publicly against Khon'Tor's earlier decision to ostracize the offspring, but they could now let her know that in their hearts, they had never supported it. Eventually, Adia, Nadiwani, and Acaraho made their way out of the Great Chamber.

Khon'Tor smiled smugly as he watched them file out. *I weathered it all. Adia is sworn to secrecy and will never reveal my crimes against her. I finally have her under my control. If it were not for this hateful female I am paired with and her seeding by another man, and the Waschini threat still on the horizon—but I cannot resolve those tonight. I need a break, however long it lasts, from the drama.*

As Acaraho walked silently beside Adia, he finally admitted to himself that he cared for her more than as her protector. Acaraho had never been paired, had never mated. He was not only physically compelling, but his calm yet strong demeanor made him even more desirable. His treatment of the males under his direction won their trust and respect, and they were loyal to him to a fault. Anyone of the females in any community would have been thrilled to be selected as a mate for him. But he had always refused the consideration of the High Council to be matched with someone.

Acaraho now realized he would never be paired.

Somewhere along the line, he had fallen in love with Adia. He knew he could never have her—that no male could. She was a Healer. But he wanted no other, and the idea of having to leave her side and take up a life with someone else was unacceptable to him. He was saddened by the idea that his role as her protector might someday end; the thought of not seeing her every day made his heart heavy.

But Acaraho had accepted his fate and resigned himself to it. He would have to find a way to be satisfied with the memory of the days he spent lying with her, holding her in his protective embrace while she was so deathly ill. He knew he could never tell her, but he hoped that in a hundred little ways she would feel his love for her, and know she was safe—that he would do everything in his power never, ever to let anything bad happen to her again.

Acaraho also realized he might never know what Khon'Tor's part had been in Adia's injury. At the end of the meeting, he had seen pass between them what he believed to be the completion of the Rah-hora. He surmised that with it Khon'Tor had bought her silence. Acaraho wanted to believe that the tension between the two had been eased by this. But in his gut, he knew another storm had to be coming.

Adia had gotten what she needed to ensure Oh'Dar's opportunity to learn Whitespeak—and more. Better than his original part of the deal, Khon'Tor had publicly stated that Adia would be given the support she needed and Oh'Dar would be provided whatever he required to make him a full member of the community. And Khon'Tor had extended his protection to the offspring.

As for the Rah-hora between her and Khon'Tor, Khon'Tor had in reality collected nothing from her. The silence he had asked for as fulfillment of her part of the Rah-hora was a silence she had already vowed to keep.

Had Adia told him she was never going to reveal his transgressions against her, he would have left the debt as yet unnamed, or named another. Now there was no further way in which the Rah-hora could harm her. She knew Khon'Tor would never default— and she had every confidence he would move mountains to make sure she was bound to keep her vow of silence.

Adia walked back with Acaraho and Nadiwani, a peaceful smile on her lips. Oddly, she felt her world was falling into place, piece by piece. Her friendship with Nadiwani had only deepened through the ordeals they had experienced recently. The presence of the Waschini offspring, Oh'Dar, had given her a chance to raise and nurture an offspring. A chance that never would have been possible in her role as Healer. And her role as Healer to the People of the High Rocks gave her the personal fulfillment she needed, tending and caring for the community she loved so much.

Adia glanced up at Acaraho, walking beside her. She was at peace when he was around; his strength comforted her, and she felt safe and protected. She remembered the two times when he had spoken directly to her. They had filled her with a happiness she did not recognize. And, oh, how his eyes pierced directly into her soul. She realized she wanted to draw him into her world and break down the distance their different roles created. Whether that was possible or wise, she did not let herself reflect upon for long.

Her thoughts turned back to her father, the great Apenimon'Mok, Leader of the People of the Deep Valley. Adia believed he was still watching over her. Perhaps he had sent Acaraho to protect her; she did not know. But she did know that love always brought harmony, whereas evil divided. She did not doubt—however that love existed—that it was all connected through the Great Mother.

Adia suspected Nadiwani would keep her awake that night for some time yet, between discussing Khon'Tor's speech and adding to her requirements for Oh'Dar's education now the restrictions had been lifted.

She did not mind. Her life was comprised of an odd conglomeration of pieces, and rag-tag though it might be, she felt she had a circle of her own at Kthama now. Despite the hardships of the last while, despite the injustice of what Khon'Tor had done to her, she had survived.

How fortunate for Adia that a Healer's vision of her own future was often blocked and she could enjoy her brief period of peace.

Because a storm was coming.

PLEASE READ

Thank you for your interest in my writing. If you enjoyed this book, I would very much appreciate your leaving a review.

Reviews give potential readers an idea of what to expect, and they also provide useful feedback for authors. The feedback you give me, whether positive or not so positive, helps me to work even harder to provide the content you want to read.

If you would like to be notified when the other books in this series are available, or if you would like to join the mailing list, please subscribe to my monthly newsletter on my website at https://leighrobertsauthor.com/contact

Wrak-Ayya: The Age of Shadows is the first of three series in The Etera Chronicles. The next book to read after reading Khon'Tor's Wrath is:
Book Two: *The Healer's Mantle*

ACKNOWLEDGMENTS

First and foremost, to my dear husband who put up with my disappearance from our life while I worked on this series, and who tirelessly kept the wheels turning without me.

Secondly, to my beta readers, family, and friends who joined with me in making this series a reality; your advice and support meant the world to me.
To my friends and colleagues at SPS, I thank you for the wisdom you so selflessly shared, for your encouragement, and the high standards you set. I could not leave out Ramy Vance, you are a great coach, and your insights, experience, and reassurances were invaluable.

Lastly, and not at all least, to my remarkable, wonderful, talented editor Joy Sephton—who put up with my incessantly incorrect use of lay, laid, lain, lie, as well as dealing with other grammatical blocks that I have yet to overcome. I can say without a doubt that this series is the best it could be because of her gentle, humorous, and indispensable advice. Pick out your red dress, Joy—we are on our way!

Made in the USA
Las Vegas, NV
25 September 2023

78139206R00184